SUICIDE TRAIL

The trail to the gold fields of California was full of expected dangers and unexpected disasters. Tom Brent offered the drovers good money to trail a hundred head of horses through Indian territory to the golden land, but everyone in Westport Landing knew that driving horses through Indian territory was suicide. But with the help of gold-hungry prospectors and a pack of dogs, Brent had to get those horses through to California to the Brent Brothers' stage line and neither business rival Oker Patzel nor Indian raiders were going to stop him . . .

SUICIDE TRAIL

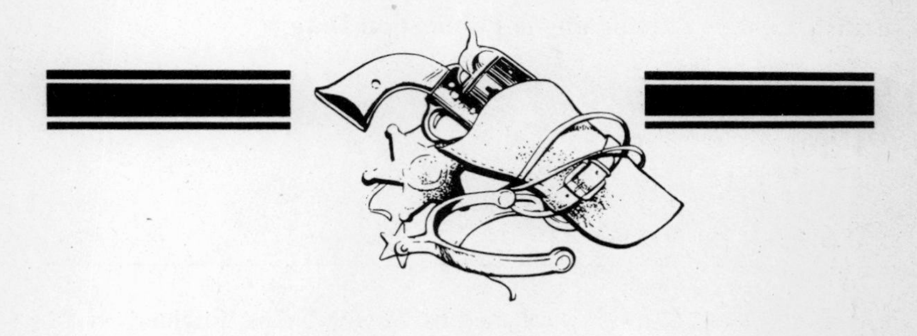

Wayne C. Lee

ATLANTIC LARGE PRINT
Chivers Press, Bath, England.
John Curley & Associates Inc.,
South Yarmouth, Mass., USA.

Library of Congress Cataloging in Publication Data

Lee, Wayne C.
Suicide trail.

(Atlantic large print)
1. Large type books. I. Title.
[PS3523.E34457S85 1989] 813′.54 88–25619
ISBN 1–55504–737–8 (pbk.: lg. print)

British Library Cataloguing in Publication Data

Lee, Wayne C., *1917–*
Suicide trail
I. Title
813′.54 [F]

ISBN 0–7451–9434–6

This Large Print edition is published by Chivers Press, England, and John Curley & Associates, Inc, U.S.A. 1989

Published by arrangement with Donald MacCampbell, Inc

U.K. Hardback ISBN 0 7451 9434 6
U.S.A. Softback ISBN 1 55504 737 8

SUICIDE TRAIL

CHAPTER ONE

It was a gloomy day in Westport Landing, but the weather couldn't equal the dreariness that dampened Tom Brent's enthusiasm. The quarter-mile-long mud hole that passed for a street was filled with horses, wagons and men, slogging through the mud. Most of these men shared a common desire to reach the gold fields of California as quickly as possible. But Brent couldn't find any who wanted to help drive a herd of Morgan horses through the Indian country to the golden land.

Brent sloshed through the mud, wondering if it always rained like this along the Missouri River in the spring. Maybe if the sun would break through, men would snap out of their dismal mood and be more receptive to Brent's offer of a fast trip across the prairies and mountains plus good wages.

Brent turned into a store with dry goods and groceries on one side and a rough plank bar on the other. Mud fell off his boots, to be trampled into the hard layer already caked there. Waiting for him at the far end of the bar was a fair-skinned, sandy-haired man whose grin did a little to brighten the murky room.

'Find anybody?' the man asked.

Brent shook his head. 'Everybody says it's suicide to try to take a herd of Morgan horses through Indian country.'

'I'll agree that it may be interesting.'

Brent sized up this new friend, Wilbur Woodcock. Woodcock and his men had brought the hundred head of Morgans from Vermont by rail and boat to St. Louis and from there had trailed them up the Missouri River to Westport Landing.

Woodcock was of average height, but he looked tall because of his small bones and narrow shoulders. His blue eyes were always twinkling as if he had just heard a good joke. Being English, Brent thought wryly, he'd probably heard the joke before he left Vermont. His sandy moustache added age to his face, making him look more than his twenty-six years.

'Seems like there ought to be men here in Westport who would be willing to drive horses in order to get to California faster,' Brent said. 'We'll cut a wagon train's time in half.'

'Or get cut in half ourselves,' Woodcock corrected him, grinning.

'I'm glad you're going on to California with me,' Brent said. 'Wish your men were going, too.'

'No chance,' Woodcock said. 'They haven't liked anything they've seen since they left Pennsylvania.'

'I've got to have those horses in Sacramento by the middle of the summer if we're to make good on that mail contract,' Brent said. 'We bid for it on the strength of having those Morgans. They can move faster and last longer than the Mexican mustangs we've been using on our coaches.'

Woodcock suddenly nudged Brent. 'Look—coming in the door. There's a couple of footloose travelers if I've ever seen any.'

Brent looked at the men, hat brims drooping from the moisture on them. They were mud-splattered from head to foot, and both needed shaves. They were fairly tall, but one man carried thirty pounds more than his companion.

'You could cut that one fellow's backbone from the front with a two-inch knife,' Woodcock said softly. 'But if he can ride and knows anything about horses, maybe we can fatten him up a bit.'

Brent nodded and moved over to the spot where the two men had pushed up against the rough plank bar.

'Could you boys use a job?' he asked.

'We've got a job,' the thin one said. 'We're heading for the gold fields in California.'

'That's where this job will take you,' Brent said.

The thin man didn't even look around, but the other man turned dark eyes on Brent, watching him intently for a moment.

'What have you got in mind?'

'I'm trailng a hundred head of horses through for a stage company. I need drovers. We'll get there in half the time it will take a wagon train to make it.'

'If you get there at all,' the thin man said.

The other man touched his companion's arm. 'Just a minute, Al. I've heard about this trail boss. Been asking all over town for men. When are you starting?' he asked Brent.

'First thing in the morning,' Brent said. 'You'll get fifty a month, grub, and a string of horses to ride.'

'We'll take it,' the man said.

'Hold on,' the thin man objected. 'I ain't said I'd take it.'

'You're in as big a hurry to get to those gold fields as I am,' his companion said. 'We ain't going to find no faster way than this.' He turned back to Brent. 'I'm Kyle Voss. This string bean is Al Redmond.'

Brent held out his hand. 'My name is Tom Brent. My brother and I own a stage line out of Sacramento. This is Wilbur Woodcock. He brought the horses here from Vermont. He'll take you fellows out to our camp now, while I look for some more men.'

Woodcock acknowledged the introductions, then left with the two new hired hands. Brent wondered if at last his luck was changing. He was more convinced than ever a few minutes later when two men came over from a table in the corner.

'You hiring riders for a drive to California?' one asked.

Brent nodded. 'I'm trailing a herd of Morgan horses through, and I need men. Pay is fifty a month. Looking for work?'

'We're figuring on going to the gold fields, anyway,' the man said. 'Might as well get paid for the trip.'

'I'll take you out to camp,' Brent said.

'We'll have to get our gear,' the man said. 'We can meet you at the west end of town in half an hour.'

Brent agreed and watched the two men leave the saloon. His luck had indeed changed. Half an hour ago it had looked as if he wouldn't get enough men to push the herd out on the trail. He could still use another man or two, but he had enough now so that he would move out at dawn tomorrow whether he got more or not.

Brent turned to the bartender, who was idle at the moment. 'Seen any other men here today who might like a job driving horses?' he asked.

The bartender shook his head. 'I get all kinds here, but not many fools. You just corraled about all the fools I've had today.'

'You think a man's a fool to earn his way to California?'

'I didn't say that,' the bartender denied, picking up a rag and wiping at a damp spot on the plank. 'A job as wagon boss or guide or even camp flunky wouldn't be so bad. But it's plain suicide to try to drive good horses through Indian territory.'

'I've heard that before,' Brent admitted, knowing he couldn't say much to put down that argument. 'But the Indians aren't on the warpath now.'

'They don't have to be on the warpath to steal horses,' the bartender said. 'Fact is, they can do a better job when they ain't on the warpath. Nobody is watching them so close then.'

'I'll be watching them plenty close,' Brent said. 'They may get away with one or two horses, but that's no reason to be afraid to go on the drive.'

'They ain't going to be satisfied with just one or two horses likes them Morgans. You lift a finger to stop them, and they'll fill you so full of arrows, you'll look like a pincushion. You mark my words, you ain't going to get them horses to California. If the Indians don't kill you and steal the herd, some white men will. Horses like that are worth more than gold out there on that prairie.'

Brent went outside. Talk like the bartender's would discourage any potential trail hand who happened to hear him. He was surprised to find that it was almost dark. Under these low clouds, it would be inky black in twenty minutes. He'd better get out to the meeting place. He'd hate to lose his new hired hands just because he couldn't find them in the dark.

The street was still full of wagons and teams and men. The mud, churned to the consistency of thick soup, sucked at wheels, hoofs and boots and splashed man and beast with equal disregard. Watching the scene, Brent's attention was drawn to a rider on the far side of the street. Something about the way he slumped in the saddle seemed familiar.

The man was past him, riding away through the mud, when it struck him who the man might be. The only man he knew who rode like that was Oker Patzel. He tried to run up the walk to get a closer look at the rider but the heavy foot traffic stopped him and turned him back.

Wheeling to the hitchrack where he had left his horse, he mounted and pushed his horse after the rider. But the traffic in the street was just as congested as it had been on the sidewalk. He spent agonizing minutes trying to get around loaded wagons that were struggling through the mud, their drivers cursing and cracking their whips.

He had to find out if that was Patzel. It surely couldn't be, he told himself. Oker Patzel was Frank Shopay's right-hand man and he should be in California now, helping

Shopay plan the downfall of the Brent Brothers' stage line. It was Shopay who was bidding against Tom and Bill Brent for the new mail contract to Columbia. Both had stage lines running there now, but the one who got the mail contract would be in a position to cut passenger rates and put the other one out of business in a hurry. Shopay was the kind who would do just that. If Oker Patzel was in Westport, it would be to get those horses.

Brent worked his way to the end of the street, but there was no sign of the rider. He had had plenty of time to get wherever he was going while Brent was mounting his horse and struggling through the congested traffic.

With a sigh, Brent reined back. Tom and Bill Brent had been very careful not to let any hint of what they were doing leak out. Brent had brought only Morrie Zimmerman, a twenty-year-old stable boy, with him. Morrie was the kind nobody in Sacramento would miss. To explain Brent's absence, they had spread the story that he was going back East to visit a sister in Ohio.

Brent hoped to get the horses to Sacramento before Shopay found out about it. The mail contracts were let out not to the lowest bidder but to the company that could promise the fastest delivery of the mail. With the Morgan horses, the Brents would have a definite edge over all competition.

Turning his horse down the main street leading west out of town, Brent pushed through the mud past the last house and reined up. Behind him, the town was fading into the darkness. He was glad he didn't have to live there. Even the permanent buildings were not the kind that offered comfortable living.

It wasn't raining now, but the clouds still hung low, blanketing the town. Lights appeared in many windows and doors as work went on outfitting wagons for the trail. That was the only excuse for the town's sudden growth, but it was a valid one. Dozens of wagons, some carrying families and their belongings and some loaded only with men burning with gold fever, pulled out of Westport Landing every day. People faced west, their eyes so glazed with wild dreams of wealth and happy homes that they couldn't see the endless miles of burning prairie and rough mountain trails between them and their goals.

Brent wasn't blind to the hardships ahead. He had just come over that trail, bucking the early spring traffic heading west as he neared the Missouri. But he had a surer promise of fortune at the end of the trail than any of these emigrants and gold seekers outfitting here in the mud.

The plopping, sucking sound of horses moving through the mud nearby reached

Brent's ears, overriding the subdued rumble of noise coming from the lighted buildings in town and the barking of dogs both back in town and out in the camps to the west and northwest. Brent waited, not moving, the possibility of Patzel's presence in Westport tempering his impatience with caution.

The horses came on. Brent could hear them distinctly now, but he still couldn't see them. His hand moved to the butt of the pistol he had carried in the belt of his pants all day. Westport was just not the kind of a town a man wandered through unarmed.

Two riders materialized out of the gloom, and Brent relaxed as he recognized the men he had hired earlier. Then suddenly, as the two men reined up, more riders charged past them, coming straight at Brent.

'They made us come!' one of the men Brent had hired yelled as he yanked his horse to one side.

Brent tried to jerk the pistol out of his belt, but one of the horses crashed into his horse, sending him staggering backward. Brent saw the mask over the lower part of the man's face and wondered fleetingly why the man had taken the precaution to cover his face on a dark night. Brent had the sinking feeling he wasn't going to get out of this alive to tell anyone who it was, anyway.

Two other masked riders charged up against Brent's horse now. One man grabbed his arm, then jerked the gun out of his belt. Another man tossed a rope over his head and yanked the loop tight, pinning his arms to his sides.

Brent looked around for the men he had hired back in town, but they were gone. Only the plopping of their horses' feet in the mud came out of the night as they raced toward town.

Not a man spoke a word, and Brent wondered if they were afraid of giving their identity. He couldn't think of three men in the whole town that he knew, outside of his own crew. Of course, one of these men might be Patzel.

One man kicked his horse up ahead of Brent and grabbed the reins from Brent's saddle horn. As he led the horse farther away from town, Brent toyed with the idea of making a break. But he knew he had no chance. One man was leading his horse; another held the rope that pinned Brent's arms to his side. Even if Brent succeeded in breaking away, the man with the rope would jerk him out of his saddle.

After several hundred yards, one of the men broke the silence. 'To the right,' he growled. 'There's a gully there. That will take us past those camps.'

The man leading Brent's horse reined off the muddy road to the right. The lights of town were still visible behind. Off to the left were a dozen campfires, making the campsite of a wagon train getting ready to head west, probably at dawn tomorrow. Farther to the left were a half-dozen other fires, pinpointing a smaller camp. But directly ahead it was pitch black.

Fury began building up in Brent as he contemplated his helplessness. He didn't mind a fight, even against heavy odds, as long as he could deal out a fair share of punishment to his tormentors. But to be tied up like a calf at branding time made his blood pound through his head like a hammer.

'Here's the gully,' the lead rider said, reining up. 'Where do we get down to the bottom?'

If he was ever going to make a break, Brent decided, it had to be before he was taken into that gully. Working a hand up under the rope around his middle, he tried to loosen it enough to jerk it over his head. The man holding the rope apparently felt the movement, because the rope suddenly snapped tight, and Brent was jerked backward out of the saddle. He barely had time to kick his feet free of the stirrups before he was yanked over the rump of his horse, to fall heavily on the wet grass.

There was a moment then while the man dismounted, and the rope around him slackened. Although he had the wind partly knocked out of him by the fall, fury drove him to yank at the rope, jerking it up over his head. He rolled to his knees just as a man approached, stooping over him. Rearing up, he drove his shoulder into the man's belly. Breath whistled out of the man's lungs as he reeled backward.

'He's still got fight in him,' one of the other men exclaimed. 'I'll take care of that.'

'Hold it!' the third man snapped. 'As still as it is tonight, everybody in town and these camps would hear that gun. We've got to keep this quiet.'

They moved in then, one from either side, while the man Brent had hit came charging at him from the front, wild curses bubbling from him. Brent had to judge where they were in the darkness more by sound than sight.

He struck out with all the force he had, but his breath was still painfully short and his blows lacked the power he ordinarily possessed. One fist hit him in the side, and he retaliated, knowing the satisfaction of feeling his fist rip skin away from bone.

Then he was hit from two other angles, and he couldn't strike back fast enough or hard enough to inflict any real damage. Frustration poured thorugh him, hurting more than the pain of the blows. Retreat was something he had never learned, so he concentrated on the man ahead of him and charged forward, driving fists into his face until the man reeled backward, barely able to stay on his feet.

Then a blow caught Brent on the back of the head, filling the night with bright lights. Struggling to keep on his feet, Brent struck out wildly, but now his fists could find no target. Another blow landed like the kick of a mule on his ear, and he felt himself going down in spite of his fierce will to stand.

He was barely aware of hitting the ground. He heard the voices of the men as if they were in some far-off dream. One man knelt to touch him, but he had no strength to resist.

'He ain't moving,' the man said softly. 'I think he's dead. You said we'd just hold him till you could get the horses.'

'I didn't figure on killing him,' another man said. 'But maybe it's better this way. Let's toss him in the gully. With him out of the way permanently, the rest will be easy.'

Brent was barely aware of being moved and of the falling sensation as he went over the rim of the gully. Mud and grass got in his mouth and nostrils as he tumbled down a steep slope. He came to rest in a soggy patch of grass with a half-inch of water oozing round his body. Then blackness, even deeper than the night, moved down on him.

CHAPTER TWO

Tom Brent's first realization that he was still painfully alive came when he felt a tug on his leg. He fought his way up out of a seemingly bottomless hole with excruciating slowness. A sharp pain in his leg brought him back to full consciousness. The night was still as black as the bottom of a well, but the pain had shredded the mantle that had cut him off from reality.

When he hunched his shoulders off the ground, pain shot through his neck and head. There was another tug at his leg, and he pulled it back. At the movement, a snarl cut through the darkness.

The sound brought Brent to a sharp awareness of his surroundings. He was being attacked by some animal, and his leg had already been bitten a time or two. He had no idea what time it was. He was lying in a half-inch of water and mud, and that brought back the memory of how he had been thrown into the ravine.

Trying to sit up, he jerked his leg back under him. More snarls came out of the darkness, and Brent realized there were several animals in the gully with him. He thought of the two dogs that Wilbur Woodcock had brought from Vermont with him. They were shepherds and were especially trained to work with horses. They would never attack a man, dead or alive, unless it was in defense of the horse herd, so it couldn't be those dogs.

One animal lunged forward and snapped at Brent, ripping his sleeve. It came close enough to Brent's face so that he could see it was a dog, probably from one of the emigrant camps. But knowing they were dogs wasn't going to help Brent much unless he could stand up like a man and order them back to their wagons, and he couldn't do that.

When the dogs began inching forward again, Brent tried to shout at them. His voice was barely a whisper. He couldn't see the dogs, but he could hear them as they hesitated at the sound of his whisper. He knew that hesitation was only temporary, though. They were obviously starving, and no whisper was going to override that hunger.

One of the dogs dived at him, then lunged backward as Brent surged upward, finding his strength returning rapidly. He managed to reach a sitting position with both hands behind him to hold him up.

Suddenly a dancing light appeared on the rim of the gully a hundred feet away. The dogs, gathering encouragement from the light, set up a clamor. One of them dived at Brent, and he yelled, his voice a few notches above a whisper this time

The light stopped dancing for a moment, then began cutting big arcs in the night as it moved rapidly along the rim of the gully to a spot directly above Brent. There it stopped, throwing a faint glow into the gully. Brent could see the four dogs now. Two were small and two were huge, all lean and obviously hungry, their eyes glowing in the reflected light of the lantern.

Brent yelled again as the two smaller dogs made another pass at him. On the rim above, there was a babble of frightened children's voices. At any moment, Brent expected the youngsters to turn and run, leaving the dogs to worry him to death.

Finally one of the youngsters called sharply, 'What have you found, Bowser?'

The voice seemed to renew the courage of the dogs, for they growled louder, and both small dogs dived at Brent again. He yelled louder than before, and this time the youngsters heard and understood.

'It's somebody!' one exclaimed. 'Bowser, get back.'

The lantern started descending the slope like a falling star as the youngsters slid down to the bottom of the gully. The boy with the lantern hit the bottom first and regained his balance, still holding the lantern at arm's length.

'Get back!' he ordered, and the dogs obeyed. 'It's a man,' he said to his two companions.

Another boy crowded up beside the first one. 'Who are you, mister? What are you doing here?'

'I've got some horses south of here,' Brent said, his voice little more than a whisper again now that he wasn't trying to shout. 'Some men want those horses and tried to kill me.'

'Gee!' the boy with the lantern exclaimed. 'Good thing our dogs found you. We were out hunting coons. Pa said there should be some this close to the river.'

'We can't leave him here,' the littlest youngster said. 'Something worse than our dogs might find him.'

'Let's take him back to camp. Ma will know what to do with him. Can you walk?'

'I doubt it, without help,' Brent said. 'I couldn't even keep your dogs away.'

'They're hungry,' one boy said. 'Ma said we shouldn't bring Bowser along, but Pa said we needed him. They ended up by agreeing to bring him, but he was to hunt his own grub. Reckon he figured on eating you.'

'He had that in mind, all right,' Brent said.

With two of the boys helping him, he managed to get to his feet. His head seemed about to burst, and the region of the gully that was visible in the lantern light whirled and dipped in front of his eyes.

Painfully, Brent moved along the gully to a place where the sides fell away to a gentle slope. With the boys helping him, he got to the top. From there he saw the fires of the train not far away.

With the boys steadying him, he moved across the uneven prairie to the nearest of the campfires. The four dogs trotted along on either side, nosing out every scent, no matter how old it was.

One of the boys yelled for his mother, and a woman and a teen-age girl came to the edge of the circle of firelight. They took charge of Brent while they listened to the boys' explanation of how they had found him.

'First we've got to wash off the mud and see how bad he is hurt,' the older woman said. 'Then we'll patch him as best we can. In the morning, we'll take him into town and leave him with a doctor.'

By the time the two women had finished cleaning him up and doctoring his cuts and bruises, Brent was feeling almost human again. Except for a bad bump on the head, he was sure there was nothing seriously wrong with him. He'd be stiff and sore for a while, but rest would do as much for him as any doctor could.

The women wanted to put Brent to bed in the wagon, but he refused. He had already made up his mind that he'd slip away before dawn and get back to his own camp. Whoever had tried to kill him tonight would probably try to steal the horse herd now. He had to alert his men to the danger.

Brent's sleep was fitful. He had a dozen bad bruises that ached and throbbed and kept him from sleeping much. He was wide awake when the first tints of dawn brightened the northeastern sky. During the night, the clouds had rolled away, and Brent guessed that the day was going to be bright and steaming hot as the ground gave up some of the moisture it had received the day before.

Slipping quietly out of his borrowed blankets, he painfully pulled on his boots and moved out of the wagon camp. He wasn't positive where his camp was, because his directions had become thoroughly muddled during the night's action.

He was a quarter of a mile from the camp when the light got strong enough for him to get his bearings. His guess as to the direction to his camp hadn't been far off.

Brent pushed along, wondering if the thieves had already struck. If not, they surely would soon. If he had been right in identifying that rider in town as Oker Patzel, then he'd bet that Patzel was behind this whole thing.

The rising sun found Brent moving slowly and painfully over a small hill, hoping the horse herd would be on the other side. But it wasn't and he hadn't come in sight of it yet when a rider appeared on a ridge to Brent's left and quickly swung toward him. Brent felt a wave of helplessness sweep over him. He not only was afoot; he was without a weapon of any kind.

Then he recognized the Englishman, Wilbur Woodcock. Turning toward him, he tried to hurry, but his aching muscles refused to respond. Woodcock pulled up beside him.

'Where have you been?' he demanded. 'What happened to you?'

Brent explained what had taken place since he had sent Woodcock back to camp last night with the new hands, Voss and Redmond, and ended with a question: 'Are the horses all right?'

'Sure. Any reason they shouldn't be?'

'Whoever jumped me must figure on getting the horses. What other reason could they have for trying to kill me?'

Woodcock nodded. 'That makes sense. Can you ride if I swing you up behind me?'

'Sure,' Brent said. 'I want to get back to the herd fast.'

The jolt of the horse was pure misery to Brent, but he gritted his teeth and hung on as Woodcock guided the horse toward camp. Relief mingled with his discomfort when Brent saw the horse herd grazing contentedly a short distance from the spot where Morrie Zimmerman had set up his chuck wagon. The wagon carried bedrolls and everything else that the man would need on the drive.

Two men were riding slowly around the

horses as they grazed. Woodcock's two shepherd dogs were with the riders, sometimes trotting at the heels of the saddled horses, sometimes lying in the grass, mouths open, tongues hanging out. Each dog was worth three riders, Woodcock insisted. If one of the Morgans decided to leave the herd, it would take a mighty fast horse to turn him, because the rider would have to overtake the escaping horse, and the loose horse would have the added advantage of not having to carry a burden. The dogs, however, could outrun any horse in the herd for a short distance. And they knew their job well.

Not only were they good herders; they were also good watchdogs. At night, if a prowler came near the herd, the dogs would locate him and alert the night guards. Woodcock had quickly convinced Brent that he needed the dogs on the trail to California.

'Got a horse in that herd I can ride?' Brent asked as Woodcock helped him slide off to the ground.

'I don't figure you can ride anything right now,' Woodcock said.

'I've got to,' Brent said. 'If some people wanted me out of the way just so they could take the horses with less of a fight, they are probably watching the herd right now. I've got to let them know I'm here and ready to fight for the herd.'

Woodcock frowned for a moment, then

nodded. 'If you've got it figured right, just seeing you back in the saddle might change their minds. I'll cut out one of the best horses in that herd. I topped some of them myself, so I know the good ones.'

He rode off toward the herd, while Brent moved over to the wagon. After explaining to Morrie what had happened, he asked for one of the extra guns they carried.

'They took my horse and my gun,' he said. 'I guess they didn't figure I'd ever be using either one again.'

Morrie brought out a gun, and Brent shoved it into his waistband, then thought better of it and asked for a gun belt. He'd be carrying that gun all the time on the trail. He didn't want the muzzle gouging his belly all the way across the continent.

By the time Brent had the gun belt on and the gun settled in the holster, Woodcock came back with a long-legged chestnut gelding.

'This horse will go as fast and as far as anything you've ever laid eyes on,' Woodcock said proudly.

Brent had brought only one extra saddle to start the trek west. He got it now from among the supplies, and Woodcock put it on the chestnut Morgan. Brent decided he'd better get a couple more.

Swinging up on the horse, Brent clutched the saddle horn and held on for a minute until the world stopped spinning. He was much steadier than he had been when he had left the wagon camp that morning, but he was far from ready to hit the trail with the horse herd.

Riding out to the herd, he made a slow circle around it. One of the dogs came over and trotted along behind his horse. It amazed Brent how these horses accepted the dogs. Woodcock had said the dogs had been with the horses for months and could drive the horses as well as men on horseback. Yet if a strange dog should appear, the horses would go wild.

Brent stayed in the saddlle until nearly noon. If anyone was watching the herd, he surely would be aware now that Brent was back. When Brent got to the wagon, he was fairly reeling in the saddle. Dismounting, he sat down against a wagon wheel while one of the men took care of the chestnut.

'Doesn't appear to me like we'll be starting out for a day or two,' Morrie said.

'I'll have to steady down a bit,' Brent admitted. 'But we'll go as soon as possible.'

He spent the afternoon stretched out in the shade of the wagon, trying to ease the throbbing ache of his many bruises. He'd have to be at his best when he put this herd on the trail, and that would mean at least another day's lay-over. Impatience prodded him. He couldn't afford another day of idleness. Yet he couldn't afford to start out before he was able to take command, either.

Six of Woodcock's men who had helped bring the horses to Westport from Vermont came out to camp that night before starting back East the next day. Brent moved over to them and tried to stir up the gold fever that was dormant in most men. Having been to the California gold fields many times, he had no trouble describing the tantalizing phases of prospecting while passing lightly over the drudgery, mud and discomfort he had seen along the rivers.

Two of the men yielded to Brent's persuasion and agreed to sign on to drive the horses to California, but the others had seen all they wanted of the world west of the Ohio River. With those two, Brent would have a crew of seven, counting himself and Morrie Zimmerman, who would be driving the wagon. Along with the dogs, that should be enough to handle the herd.

Brent posted guards around the herd through the night, but the herd wasn't molested. At breakfast, Al Redmond, one of the first men he had hired at Westport, sat down beside Brent.

'I saw a strange rider out close to the herd last night,' he reported. 'The dog spotted him first.'

'Did you find out what he was after?' Brent asked quickly.

'Didn't get a chance. As soon as he saw me coming toward him, he kicked up the grass getting out of there. I got pretty close, though. He was riding a gray horse, if my eyes weren't playing tricks on me in the starlight. Sure didn't look like any of the Morgans.'

'Did he talk to the other guard?'

Redmond shook his head. 'Voss was out there with me. He said he didn't even see him.'

Brent finished his breakfast and went over to talk to Woodcock. Woodcock suggested that Brent forget about the rider and get ready to hit the trail. But Brent was unconditionally committed to getting the horses to Sacramento, and he had the feeling he'd better do something about the rider on the gray horse before they left the comparative safety of the town and the camps here.

'I'm going to check the camps for a gray horse,' Brent said. 'Want to come along?'

'If you're gallivanting around, I might as well go along,' Woodcock said, shaking his head in disapproval.

There were three camps pitched west of town, and Brent and Woodcock started with the closest one. It was at the second camp, however, that Brent spotted a sleek gray horse with long legs and a deep chest that suggested both speed and endurance.

The camp was swarming with people repacking wagons, eliminating things the wagon boss said they couldn't take, and making last-minute repairs. Brent threaded his way through the people to the wagon boss.

'Who does that gray horse belong to?' Brent asked after he had introduced himself. He pointed to the gray standing beside a wagon halfway across camp.

The wagon boss shrugged. 'I don't have the slightest idea. I don't know half the people in this camp yet, let alone their horses. After we get strung out for a few days on the trail, I can tell you who everybody is and what belongs to him.'

'I'd like to talk to the man who owns that horse,' Brent said.

The wagon boss went with Brent and Woodcock to the wagon where the horse stood. But no one there knew anything about him. Brent worked his way around the camp, asking about the horse. No one knew the horse, and finally, when Brent turned to point out the gray to one man, he discovered that the horse was gone.

Brent searched the camp quickly, then rode outside. There was a ravine a short distance from the camp, and Brent guessed that the rider had taken the gray horse down this and maybe on to town.

'We might ride into town and look,' Brent

suggested.

Woodcock shook his head. 'Wouldn't do any good. Now that he knows we're looking for him, he's not going to be trapped again, even in town.'

Brent agreed and turned reluctantly back toward his own camp. He ached in every joint, but he couldn't delay the start west any longer.

It was nearly noon when Brent and Woodcock got back to camp, but dinner wasn't even started. Brent reined up at the wagon.

'What's going on?' he demanded.

Morrie Zimmerman held up two pieces of paper. 'Look at these,' he fairly shouted. 'Woodcock's men found them in their bedrolls.'

Brent took the papers and read one of them aloud to Woodcock. 'Get off this drive, or you'll never live to see Fort Laramie.' Brent looked to Morrie. 'Who put these notes in the bedrolls?'

'I don't know,' Morrie said, his voice shrill with rage. 'If I could find him, I'd skin him alive. These boys were riding guard while we had breakfast, you know. They found the notes when they came in.'

'Where are they now?'

'They pulled out. Said they didn't want gold that bad. They figure on catching up with their buddies going back east.'

Brent frowned. This cut his crew to five men and two dogs. But whether he had five men or two, he had to get on the trail at dawn tomorrow.

CHAPTER THREE

When dinner was over and the dishes washed up, Brent sent Morrie out to relieve Woodcock at the herd. Woodcock's two dogs were not out with the horses now but lounging around the wagon in the shade. Morrie would keep an eye on the horses this afternoon, but he wouldn't be asked to ride night guard.

Woodcock came in and swung out of the saddle at the wagon where Brent had seated himself, aching in every joint.

'Without more men, we may not be able to handle this drive,' he said.

Brent squinted up at him. 'Why not? The horses aren't wild.'

'Oh, they're gentle enough,' Woodcock said quickly. 'They're all green broke or better, and they're used to the trail now. It isn't the driving that's worrying me. It's at night that we'll have trouble. Out there just now, a coyote could have stolen that herd from me if it had been dark.'

'We'll keep more than one man on guard at

night,' Brent said.

'We don't have enough men to do the job right. We need more guard duty at night than we do to drive during the day.'

Brent nodded. 'I know that. But we haven't got them. I'm depending a lot on those dogs of yours.'

'They will be a great help,' Woodcock said, 'but only as a warning. They can't do much to fight off thieves.'

'A warning from the dogs will bring out all the men we have.'

Woodcock stared at the horses. 'I've been doing some thinking out there. If somebody is planning to jump us and take the herd, he aims to keep us short-handed. That's why my boys got those notes.'

Brent nodded. 'I figured that out a long time ago. They'll hit somewhere between here and Fort Laramie. My brother Bill said he'd have some extra men at Fort Laramie to help me drive the horses across the high country. He may even be in the crew himself. But between here and Fort Laramie, we're going to be short-handed.'

'My boys were good drovers but not much on fighting,' Woodcock said. 'When do I go back on guard?'

'You and I will take the first shift tonight,' Brent said. 'I'll have to go into town this afternoon and get a couple more saddles and more ammunition.'

'Want me to come along?'

'Thought I'd take Al Redmond and let you rest,' Brent said.

Brent checked everything in the wagon, making a list of the extra supplies he had decided he needed. He'd thought he was ready for the trail, but the way things had been happening since the horses arrived, he had revised his thinking.

While he was in town with Al Redmond, he considered asking around for more men, but he doubted if he'd find many he hadn't contacted a couple of days ago.

Back at camp, he readied everything for a dawn start on the morrow. As sundown neared, he discovered that Woodcock wasn't in camp. Worry tugged at him. Whoever had hidden those warning notes last night might still be at work, picking off Brent's crew one by one so he couldn't start on the trail at all.

Brent asked Kyle Voss, who was loafing around camp trying to catch some extra sleep, if he had seen Woodcock. But he hadn't seen him since he'd flopped down on his blankets shortly after Brent and Redmond left for town.

Saddling up, Brent started towards town to look for Woodcock, then suddenly changed his direction. He recalled some of Woodcock's men hoorawing him the first day they'd gotten here about his weakness for pretty women. There had been some unusually pretty girls in that wagon train they'd visited this morning.

Brent put his chestnut Morgan to a lope, although the jolt threatened to split his head. He aimed toward the train, which was preparing to pull out tomorrow morning. If he didn't find Woodcock there, he'd go back to town.

Before he reached the camp, however, Brent saw the shiny black Morgan that Woodcock rode standing at the wheel of one of the canvas-covered wagons. He found Woodcock not far away, visiting with a family of emigrants around a supper fire. It didn't surprise him in the least that one member of that family was a pretty girl in her late teens.

Brent tipped his hat to the ladies but didn't dismount. 'Did you forget that we're riding herd tonight?' he asked Woodcock.

Woodcock sighed. 'Time got away from me.' He spoke to the girl. 'Since we're all heading west in the morning, perhaps we'll meet again.'

Brent doubted that, but he didn't say anything. By tomorrow night, he hoped to have twice as many miles behind the horse herd as this train would be able to cover.

Back at camp, Brent and Woodcock ate some cold meat sandwiches; then Woodcock whistled to the two dogs and rode out with Brent to the herd, the dogs following obediently. Behind them, Redmond and Voss were complaining because they had to eat a cold supper.

It was dusk when Brent and Woodcock relieved Morrie at the herd. Each took one dog with him and began a slow ride around the grazing animals. Brent looked at the horses admiringly. They were the prettiest horses he had ever seen. There were just three colors in the herd, black, chestnut and bay. The horses were all about the same size, around a thousand pounds and about fourteen hands high. That made a nice-sized riding horse that was still big enough for all harness jobs except heavy draft work.

The night was clear, and nothing disturbed the peacefulness. At dawn, Brent had his camp stirring. Before the sun was up, the wagon moved out, with Morrie on the seat. Brent and his three riders and two dogs got the herd moving to the west.

Brent pushed the horses to the north of the regular trail. There was good grass there for the horses to nibble on as they moved along, and he wanted to keep them clear of the emigrant trains traveling on the regular trail. He certainly didn't need the confusion that would result if his animals got mixed up with those of the trains.

For two days they moved on at a rapid pace. Each morning a new team was hitched to the wagon that Morrie was driving. Brent had a double purpose in that. It helped take the edge off some of the green broke Morgans so they would be ready for use on the coaches in his stage line, and it also made it possible for Morrie to keep the wagon up with the herd. One team, having to pull the wagon every day at that pace with no time for grazing, would soon drop from exhaustion.

The third night out, Woodcock suggested that they leave one dog in camp while the other went with the night riders.

'Even the dogs are going to wear out at this pace,' he said. 'They have to trot along all day, then watch the herd all night. Let them take turns working at night, too. One dog out there should be enough to spot any trouble.'

Brent agreed.

At dawn, Brent made his usual count of the horses before pushing them out on the trail. This morning he discovered he was two short. He counted a second time before telling Woodcock. Woodcock quickly checked the herd.

'Two bays are missing,' he reported. 'I know how many of each color there are supposed to be.'

Brent frowned. 'I didn't expect Indians to bother us this close to the river. And if it was white men, they would surely have taken a dozen, at least, while they were at it.'

'It almost has to be some white man,' Woodcock said. 'Maybe he figured we wouldn't miss just two.'

'What are we going to do about it?' Voss asked.

'Go after them,' Brent said. 'We can't afford to lose any. Wilbur and I will look for the strays. You three stay with the herd.'

Once they were away from the herd, Woodcock said, 'They didn't stray away. If they had, whoever was riding guard would have spotted them when he rode around the herd. Those horses were led away fast enough to be out of sight when the guard came by.'

'Funny the dog didn't hear or see anything,' Brent said.

'Reckon we're going to have to keep both dogs out there,' Woodcock decided. 'Whoever got those horses must have seen the dog and waited until he was on the far side of the herd before grabbing the two bays.'

'We may be riding right into a trap,' Brent suggested.

Woodcock nodded. 'That's possible. From what Morrie told me of this Shopay you're bucking out in Sacramento, there's hardly a limit to what he'll do to keep the upper hand.'

'Shopay isn't supposed to know we're bringing in these horses.'

'You don't really believe that your secret hasn't leaked out, do you?'

Brent shook his head. 'I'm sure it has. I think that rider on the gray horse is Oker Patzel.'

'Maybe he stole the two horses last night,'

Woodcock said.

'Maybe,' Brent conceded. 'And maybe someone from one of these emigrant trains needed a couple of horses real bad. We'll look at any camps along the trail first.'

'There was a train going into camp last night just about even with us,' Woodcock said.

They were barely in sight of the camp, which was just breaking up in preparation for moving out, when Woodcock stood in his stirrups and pointed to a wagon on the near side of camp.

'Look at those bays,' he exclaimed. 'They're Morgans.'

Brent didn't even look for the wagon boss. Angling his chestnut toward the wagon, he reined up sharply, Woodcock beside him.

'Where did you get that team?' he asked the stoop-shouldered man who was fitting harness to one of the bays.

The man came out from behind the horse and stared at Brent and Woodcock. He was tall and thin and dirty, with a gray beard and faded blue eyes. A woman came around from the back of the wagon where two old horses stood, their heads drooping. They were so thin their ribs threatened to poke through their hides.

'What's the trouble, Jase?' she demanded in a shrill voice.

'Visitors, Em,' the man said. 'Asking about

our team.'

After a long silence, Brent leaned over the horn of his saddle. 'I'm still asking.'

'I bought them in Westport,' the man said.

'You didn't buy a team like that in Westport,' Woodcock snapped.

'What about those old crowbaits back there?'

'I'm going to plow with them when I get to Oregon.'

'They'll never make it to Oregon even if they don't have to stretch a tug,' Brent said. 'But that doesn't give you a right to steal my horses.'

'I didn't steal any horses,' the man shouted, and people from the wagons on either side came over to listen.

'You didn't buy them,' Brent said.

'I ain't no thief!' the man yelled, but Brent could see the fear in his eyes.

'Go away and leave us alone,' the woman screamed.

Brent turned to a boy about ten years old who was watching with bulging eyes. 'Sonny, did these people have these horses yesterday?'

The boy shook his head. 'I ain't ever seen them before. They used those old horses yesterday, and they got 'way behind. Mr. Brewster said they'd have to go back if they couldn't keep up.'

Brent felt sorry for the old man and woman, but he couldn't let that stop him from reclaiming his horses.

'That kid don't know what he's talking about,' the man said, sweat breaking out on his forehead.

'Go ahead and tell him the truth, Jase,' the woman said in despair.

'He can't prove I stole them,' the man said.

'I've got a hundred head of Morgans out there,' Brent said, jerking a thumb over his shoulder. 'I don't see another Morgan in this camp. I'll ask your wagon boss if you started out from Westport with these horses.'

The man was trembling now, and his shoulders sagged forward. 'All right. So I borrowed them. I had to have them or turn back.'

'I didn't want to come in the first place,' the woman said. 'We're too old to make a new start out in Oregon. I told Jase that, but he wouldn't listen. Now maybe we can go back.'

The man wheeled angrily on his wife. 'They hang horse thieves out here,' he snapped.

'All I want is my horses,' Brent said.

'You can have them,' the man said, relief sweeping over his face as he realized that he might get out of this without any punishment.

Brent dismounted and began unharnessing the two Morgans. He was surprised at how well the horses behaved. Woodcock had said some of the horses were green broke, others well broke. This team obviously was well broke.

'Who helped you get these horses?' Brent asked as the collars were taken off.

'I did it myself,' the man said stoutly.

Brent faced the old man. 'That's a lie and you know it. What time did you get them?'

'Why—er—this morning—almost morning,' the man stuttered.

Brent knew the truth then and looked at Woodcock, who was standing in his stirrups, looking over the camp.

'I don't see his gray horse anywhere,' Woodcock said.

'Whose gray horse?' the man asked, his face showing his surprise.

'The man who stole these horses for you,' Brent said. 'He rides a long-legged gray horse. Where is he?'

'I don't know nothing about a man on a gray horse,' the man said sullenly.

Brent turned to the youngster, who was still standing close by, his mouth open as he watched and listened. 'Did you see a man on a gray horse, sonny?'

The boy nodded. 'He ate supper with them last night. And I saw somebody over here just before getting-up time. Could have been him again.'

Brent turned to the old man. 'How about that?'

The man sighed. 'All right. So I ain't man

enough even to steal a horse. This big fellow came by last night while I was doctoring the fistula on one of my horses, and he told me he'd get me a good team to pull my wagon. All he asked was his supper, and I wasn't going to ask no questions about where he got the horses.'

'He also made you promise not to tell anybody how you got the horses,' his wife put in. 'You can't even keep a promise.'

Brent stared at the man, who was completely subdued now. 'I want you to describe that man to me.'

'He was over six feet tall and must have weighed close to two hundred,' the man said. 'Had brown hair and sort of green eyes. Do you know him?'

'Like the back of my hand,' Brent said grimly, all doubt gone now about the presence of Oker Patzel. 'He's the kind you want to stay away from.'

'We're going back home where we should have stayed,' the woman said. 'Maybe it's a blessing you came after the horses.'

Looking at the worn-out tools and machinery in and around the old wagon, Brent had to agree. That wagon would never hold together to get to Oregon, and if it did, the tools the man had would never plant and cultivate a crop.

Putting his rope on one horse while Woodcock looped his rope on the other,

Brent rode out of camp.

'Did he describe Patzel?' Woodcock asked when they were headed for their own camp.

'As well as I could have done,' Brent said. 'He's here, which means that Shopay found out what we're up to. Patzel will do everything he can to make sure we never get those horses to California.'

CHAPTER FOUR

A quarter of a mile from the camp, Brent suddenly reined up. 'I wonder if there are any young fellows in that train who would like to get to California in a hurry.'

Woodcock nodded. 'It's worth checking. I'll take the horses on to camp.'

Brent handed his rope to Woodcock and reined around toward the camp. There he found the wagon boss.

'Do you have any young men who would like to earn their way to California and make it in half the time this train will?' he asked.

The wagon boss stared at Brent for a moment, then shook his head. 'Nobody in this train will go with you,' he said. 'They're either here with a family or are too young to commit suicide.'

Brent ignored the open hostility in the man's voice and looked down the line of waiting wagons. 'There must be some men here who could use the extra money when they get there.'

'This train is going to Oregon, not California,' the wagon boss said testily. 'Anyway, everybody here figures on getting there, not being scalped on the way.'

'You've been listening to too much scare talk,' Brent said.

'Maybe, and maybe I've just seen this trail a few more times than you have. This is my third summer as wagon boss. I know these so-called friendly Indians. They're friendly as long as you share with them what you've got. But just try running them off without giving them something they want! Mister, I wouldn't take your job for all the gold in California!'

'Mind if I talk to some of the men?' Brent asked.

'I sure do mind!' the wagon boss snapped. 'When I signed on to take this train through to Oregon, I took responsibility for everyone in it. I ain't letting you talk up gold fever and coax some of them into going with you and getting killed before they get to Laramie.'

Brent reined away, riding along the line of wagons standing behind the leader, waiting for the word to move out. Looking at the faces of the men as he passed, he saw that they already knew about him and his horse drive. They stared at him as if he were a living corpse or, at best, a crazy man. The wagon boss had nothing to worry about; he couldn't have coaxed any man away from the safety of the train.

Nudging his horse into a lope, he struck out after Woodcock. The man on the gray horse, Oker Patzel, had been in that wagon camp. Evidently he had stayed long enough to spread the word about the dangers facing the horse drive. Patzel was hedging his bet, making sure Brent got no more men to help him even from the wagon trains he was passing.

So far, Patzel had appeared to be alone. But Brent would bet he had a crew of men somewhere. He'd have to have a crew to take over the herd, and Brent was positive that was what he had in mind. He must have a camp not far away. That camp would keep up with the horse herd as it moved along and would be Patzel's headquarters.

For a minute Brent toyed with a daring idea. If he could find that camp and raid it with his few men, the surprise might balance things out or even give Brent the advantage. Brent could depend on Woodcock and Morrie to help on such a raid. But what about Al Redmond and Kyle Voss? They seemed to be good drovers, but to ask them to go looking for a fight just to get the herd through might be too much.

Woodcock had the two bays back in the

herd by the time Brent reached camp. In half an hour they were on the trail.

They reached the junction of the Blue River with the Kansas and turned north, following the east bank of the Blue. The first night along the Blue, the dogs, tagging the men riding night herd, began barking. Brent, having assigned Redmond and Voss to the first shift with the herd, was just bedding down at camp. He pulled on his boots and got to his feet, listening to the dogs. Turning, he saw Woodcock getting out of his blankets.

'What would set off those dogs like that?' Brent asked.

'There's something out there that shouldn't be,' Woodcock said. 'We'd better have a look.'

Brent was already halfway to his horse, which was standing saddled but with loosened cinch. 'Won't all that racket make the horses run?' he asked, yanking up on the cinch.

'No,' Woodcock said, unconcerned. 'They've been around those dogs most of their lives. But whatever the dogs are barking at might spook them.'

Brent mounted and kicked his horse into a run toward the herd. The dogs were to the west of the herd, looking toward the river. Redmond and Voss were still at their posts, circling the horses. The Morgans didn't seem unduly alarmed, but they were looking west into the night. Brent reined up beside the tall thin man, Al Redmond.

'What do you make of it?'

'Ain't sure,' Redmond said. 'I thought once I heard a wagon creaking. But I can't figure why anybody would be out driving this time of night, especially a way off the trail like this.'

Brent nodded and listened, but the dogs were making too much racket for him to pick up any other sound. Woodcock came up and stopped to listen, too.

Brent was just ready to move out to the west when he saw something top a swell in the prairie.

'It is a wagon!' he exclaimed. 'That outfit must be lost.'

'Let's get out there and stop them,' Woodcock said quickly. 'If that wagon comes jiggling up here, these horses might spook. Even though they are used to almost everything, they haven't heard many sounds like that in the middle of the night.'

Brent nodded and nudged his horse into a lope toward the wagon, Woodcock beside him. When the driver of the wagon saw them coming, he stopped his team.

As he reined to a halt, Brent noted that the wagon wasn't in especially good shape, and the horses certainly were not equal to the ones he had back in the herd. A poor emigrant and his family, he decided quickly.

'Are you lost?' he asked.

A man and a woman were sitting on the seat. In the darkness, Brent couldn't tell how old they were. A younger woman, perhaps their daughter, poked her head out from under the canvas behind them. Suddenly two riders that Brent hadn't seen before rode out from behind the wagon.

'We're not lost,' the man on the wagon seat said in a soft weary voice. 'We were just kicked out of our wagon train.'

'Kicked out?' Woodcock exclaimed. 'Why?'

'For trying to be human beings instead of brutes,' the man said, bitterness edging his soft voice.

'I don't follow you,' Brent said after a moment.

'My husband is a missionary,' the woman explained, anger in her voice. 'He has been insisting that we should try to reach any Indians we see with the gospel. Our guide said that if we saw any Indians, we should be prepared for trouble. He has been leading us in drills in how to protect ourselves and the wagons. My husband and the guide have been arguing for some time. Tonight it reached a climax, and we were ordered out.'

'I never heard of a wagon boss ordering anybody out at night,' Brent said.

'He didn't say we had to go tonight,' the man admitted. 'But when something is done, it's done. We would only have shamed ourselves by remaining another minute with those sinners.'

'I say!' Woodcock said softly to Brent. 'We'd better see that these sin-busters get on their way.'

'I forgot to introduce myself,' the man said apologetically. 'I'm Dan Hanson, a missionary to the gold camps of California. The Lord knows they need the gospel there. This is my wife Emily, and my daughter Rosene.'

For the first time the girl came out from under the canvas as she acknowledged the introduction. It was too dark to see her features clearly, but Brent could see enough to be sure she was the prettiest girl he had been close to since he left California. He could tell from the way Woodcock sucked in his breath that he shared Brent's evaluation.

'I'm Tom Brent, and this is Wilbur Woodcock,' Brent said. 'We're driving a herd of horses through to California.'

'So I gathered,' Hanson said. 'Jake told us about your camp over here. That's why we headed this way, hoping to find a place where we could spend the night while we decide what to do.'

'You've come to the right place,' Woodcock said quickly. 'We've got plenty of room if nothing else.'

Brent frowned. Dan Hanson and his family didn't worry him, but those two riders who had pushed up beside the wagon did. He couldn't see them clearly, but they definitely did not look like missionaries to him.

'Who are your friends?' he asked bluntly, indicating the two men on the horses.

'One is Jake Closter, and the other is his brother Dickie,' Hanson said. 'They completely share my views on how to deal with the wild savage, so they stuck with me when the wagon boss threw us out.'

'Better pull over close to our wagon and make camp,' Woodcock said. 'You can decide what to do in the morning.'

'Their plans are their own business,' Brent put in sharply. He was sure that Woodcock had thrown out the invitation for the Hansons to camp there to keep Brent from suggesting that they move on.

'We take this kindly,' Hanson said. 'We don't relish camping out all alone on this prairie.'

Brent wheeled his horse and led the way in a wide circle around the herd, stopping a hundred yards from his own wagon. 'This ought to be a good place,' he said.

'This is fine,' Hanson agreed.

'Just don't do anything to spook our horses,' Brent warned.

'We'll be careful about that.'

Brent rode back toward his own wagon, Woodcock with him. He dismounted and loosened the cinch.

‘You’re plenty free with invitations to strangers,’ he said finally.

‘I figured I was going to hear about that,’ Woodcock said. ‘I was boss all the way out from Vermont. I guess I forgot I wasn’t running this show.’

‘We’re a long way from Vermont,’ Brent said, not placated much by Woodcock’s apology. ‘Out here we don’t take chances like that. Dan Hanson may be a preacher, but those two men with him aren’t.’

‘They don’t look like it,’ Woodcock admitted. ‘But Hanson seems to trust them. Say, isn’t that girl a beauty?’

‘Maybe she won’t be so pretty when the sun shines on her,’ Brent said.

But when Brent and Woodcock rode over to the Hanson wagon in the morning, she was even prettier with the sun on her face than she had been in the darkness.

‘Good morning,’ Dan Hanson greeted them cheerily.

Brent returned the greeting. ‘What are your plans now?’

‘We’ve just been discussing that,’ Hanson said. ‘Emily, Rosene and I have decided we’ll go over by the trail, wait for the next train and see if they’ll let us go along with them.’

‘You’re determined to get to California, aren’t you?’

‘Certainly,’ Hanson said. ‘We started out there because we felt called to minister to those poor souls in the gold camps. One misguided wagon boss is not going to discourage me.'

'What about your companions?' Brent said, nodding to the Closter brothers.

'They will go wherever I go,' Hanson said. 'They were not the best of men when they joined that train. But they were converted, and now they are as eager to spread the gospel as I am. They did have another idea about getting to California. Jake, come over and tell Mr. Brent what you told me.'

The bigger of the two men came over from the wagon, where he had just put down his breakfast plate. Brent got a good look at him and was astonished at his size. Jake Closter was several inches above six feet and weighed two hundred and thirty or forty pounds. His brother was a small man, at least a foot shorter and a hundred pounds lighter. Brent frowned. Never had he seen two brothers so different in size and appearance. Jake gave Brent the impression of an overgrown happy-go-lucky boy, but Dickie looked mean.

'I don't see many men over in your camp,' Jake said. 'Now Dickie and me are good wranglers. We thought maybe you could use a couple more riders, and the Hansons could come along with us. We'd get to California quicker than if we waited for a wagon train.'

Brent shot a look at Woodcock, then

turned away. Woodcock's judgment wouldn't be worth a puff of prairie breeze while he was looking at Rosene Hanson. He'd have to make this decision himself.

'I do need some more men,' he said. 'But we'll have to do something about Hanson's team. We cover twice the distance each day that a regular train does. These horses wouldn't last two days at that pace.' He turned to Dan Hanson. 'Can you handle a spirited team?'

Rosene spoke up for the first time. 'If Pa can't, I can,' she said. 'Are you thinking about a team of those horses in your herd?'

'Exactly. They're Morgans and pretty fancy steppers. Some of them are only green broke. But if we switch teams every day, you can keep up with no trouble.'

'Ma and I can do the cooking, too,' Rosene volunteered. 'Pa can drive the other wagon, and your cook can help with the horses.'

Brent nodded. Looking at Woodcock, he said, 'Go catch a gentle team of those Morgans and bring them in for the Hanson wagon.'

Grinning, Woodcock nodded. 'I'll get that bay team that Patzel stole the other night. They're well broke. I wouldn't give the lady a wild team to handle.'

He tipped his hat to Rosene and spurred his horse away at a fast gallop.

CHAPTER FIVE

Brent was only half an hour later than usual getting the herd on the move. For the first hour, he kept close to the rear of the herd, checking on the drivers of the two wagons. He found out quickly that Rosene was just as good with the reins as she had claimed to be. Dan Hanson was not nearly as capable, but he had no trouble.

At noon, Brent called a halt to let the horses rest and graze while Mrs. Hanson and Rosene cooked dinner for all the men. Even though there were ten people now to feed instead of five as before, the noon stop was shorter than it had been when Morrie was cooking.

'How do you like being kicked out of the kitchen?' Brent asked Morrie as he leaned against a wagon wheel to eat.

'I like it,' Morrie said. 'I wasn't cut out to be a nursemaid to pots and pans.'

'You can say that again,' Redmond said from the front of the wagon, where he was sitting on the doubletrees while the team grazed nearby. 'This don't taste like the grub he put out. Takes a woman's touch.'

When dinner was over and the teams hitched up again, Brent sent Redmond ahead to scout while Jake Closter and Voss kept the herd pointed after him. Dickie Closter and Morrie rode flank, and Brent and Woodcock brought up the drag. This wasn't the chore that it was on a cattle drive. Horses didn't linger behind to graze as cattle did. Brent was surprised as the herd moved out to see another rider between him and Woodcock.

'Hey!' he exclaimed. 'I thought you were driving one of the wagons.'

'Ma can handle that team without any trouble,' Rosene said. 'I like to ride, and this horse of Pa's doesn't have anything to do now that we're pulling our wagon with your Morgans.'

Woodcock reined over next to Rosene. 'This sure puts some beauty in the drive,' he said, grinning. 'A good cook and a good drover. What more could you ask?'

'I might ask you to watch that black over there,' Brent said, motioning to a sleek black that had found some succulent grass and had stopped to grab it.

'That horse won't let the herd get away without him,' Woodcock said. Nevertheless, he reined over and gave the black a shove up with the other horses.

Brent wondered how much distraction Rosene was going to cause when the crew got to know her better. Woodcock was agog already, and at noon Brent had noticed Kyle Voss casting admiring glances at her.

'I reckon you can help us just as much by

making sure the wagons keep up,' Brent said.

'I suppose you think I can't drive horses,' Rosene said sharply.

'It's not the horses I'm worried about,' Brent said.

Color flooded into her cheeks, and she glared angrily at him a moment before she whipped her horse into a gallop back to the wagons.

'That was acting like anything but a gentleman,' Woodcock said peevishly.

'Maybe you were acting more like a gentleman,' Brent said. 'But you sure forgot you were driving horses. After we get to California, you can go sit on her lap for all I care.'

Woodcock wheeled his horse and spurred him over to the other side of the herd. Brent watched him, frowning. He didn't intend to let anything disrupt the work of the drive, even if it meant infuriating Rosene Hanson and every man in his crew.

Before sundown, Redmond came galloping back to Brent. 'We're almost to the crossing,' he shouted. 'And the river is flooded all over the flat.'

Brent frowned. He had hoped to get across the Big Blue tonight and camp above the confluence of the Little Blue and the Big Blue. A flooded river would force a revision of his plans. He was well acquainted with the reports of the rivers across these plains that always seemed to flood in the spring when the wagon trains tried to cross.

'We'll have to camp on this side tonight,' Brent decided reluctantly. 'We could get the herd across, but if we had any trouble with the wagons, we might not get across before dark. We can't risk that.'

After setting up camp a mile above the regular crossing, Brent rode down to look at the river. It was completely out of its banks, pouring dirty water over great areas of rich meadow grass. When it receded, it would leave a layer of mud and slime over that grass.

Brent couldn't see any place here that invited an easy crossing. Shaking his head, he reined downstream toward the regular crossing. But here he found a big train waiting on the east bank. Looking across the river, he saw another train camped there, apparently having just completed the crossing.

If Brent used the regular crossing, trail courtesy would demand that he hold back and let the train that was there cross first. That could mean a delay of at least a day, maybe two, especially if the wagon boss waited for the water to recede a little. Brent couldn't afford such a delay. He'd have to make his crossing somewhere above here.

'You look like the condemned man who just got his first look at the scaffold,' Woodcock said uneasily when Brent reached camp.

'It's not as bad as that,' Brent said. 'But we'll have to make our crossing here. There are trains on both sides of the regular crossing.'

Uneasiness gripped those who had the responsibility of getting the wagons across the river in the morning. Brent knew from his look at the river that it wasn't going to be easy.

Supper was a quiet meal. Even the drovers, who had nothing more than the horse herd to worry about, respected the concern of the others. When supper was over, Brent sat for a while and listened to the distant roar of the river. At times, the stirring of the horses nearby covered the sound, but then it came on again, as if jealous of anything that could drown it out.

Turning away from the roar of the river, he saw Kyle Voss, a scowl on his face, staring at the wagon where Rosene and her mother were washing dishes. Brent followed his gaze and saw Woodcock there, helping with the after-supper chores and apparently enjoying it.

Brent moved toward the wagon, thinking that rivalry among the men over Rosene's favor was one thing he couldn't afford. Motioning to Rosene, he called her away from the dishpan, leaving Mrs. Hanson washing and Woodcock drying. Woodcock's face mirrored his displeasure.

'Do you want one of the men to drive your wagon across tomorrow?' Brent asked.

'No,' Rosene said quickly. 'I can handle my wagon. It's Pa I'm worried about. He's not the best driver in the world.'

Brent had long ago reached that conclusion, but he was surprised to hear Rosene admit it. The fact that he was talking to Rosene instead of her father about tomorrow's crossing was proof of his opinion of Dan Hanson's ability, Brent thought. She had the strength of the family.

'We'll take one wagon across at a time,' Brent said. 'A couple of the boys and I will ride along just in case we're needed.'

'It might give Pa some confidence if you'd let him drive his own team.'

Brent nodded, not sure that he would dare do that. 'Maybe the river will be down by morning,' he said.

He had little hope that it would be, and dawn proved his fears well grounded. He had the camp hustling as soon as it was light. With breakfast over, the men saddled up, while the women packed the wagons so that nothing that could be damaged by water was on the floors.

'We'll cross the horses first,' Brent said. 'It's wide here, but it shouldn't be so swift except in the channel. If we have no trouble with the horses, we'll bring the wagons across here, too.'

'A swimming horse ain't going to tell us much about what will happen when a wagon gets in that deep water,' Jake Closter said.

'It's the best we can do,' Brent snapped.

'This is Sunday,' Dan Hanson said. 'We ought to hold a prayer meeting, at least, before we cross.'

'You can hold a short service when we get on the other side,' Brent said.

Brent couldn't tolerate a delay now. He assigned each man to his job and sent Dan Hanson back to the wagons with his wife and daughter.

Brent rode point himself, staying downstream from the lead horses to keep them from drifting. If they allowed the current to take them far off course, they could come out close to that train that had crossed yesterday.

However, the water was shallow for a long way out into the river. Then, for a short distance, it was swift. This was the main channel, Brent decided, and it was soon crossed.

The horses made the crossing easily, swimming only when they were in the channel. The biggest threat to the wagons would be the mud on the flats on either side of the channel.

Brent took Woodcock and Al Redmond back across the river with him. The other four riders stayed to settle the herd down. Brent had decided to take Rosene's wagon across first, because he had faith in her ability to handle her team.

Rosene had the Hansons' two horses tied behind her wagon, and her saddle was on a wooden box inside the wagon bed. She spoke to the team, and the Morgans responded as if they had been obeying her voice for weeks instead of just one day. Brent had decided not to put fresh horses on the wagons this morning. The horses that had pulled the wagons yesterday would be acquainted with their job and would be more dependable for the crossing.

Rosene's wagon made the crossing without trouble. The muddy bottom on both sides of the channel forced the horses to pull hard, but the short swim presented no difficulty.

The three men went back across the river to escort Dan Hanson's wagon over. Just as they started the wagon into the water, Brent saw Rosene splash into the river from the other side. She had saddled one of the Hanson horses and was coming back to help if she was needed.

Dan Hanson proved to be no better with a team in a crisis than Brent had expected. Instead of letting the horses have their heads when they hit the swimming depth, he sawed on the reins, trying to keep them from drifting with the current. One back wheel hit something and caught there, stopping the wagon. Brent guessed it might be the snag of a tree stump.

He crowded his horse over where he could give the wagon a shove. Hanson was standing up in his wagon, yelling and tugging on the reins. When the wheel finally came loose from the snag, the wagon was pointing almost downstream, and the current caught the back end of the wagon, whipping it around so swiftly that Brent couldn't get his horse out of the way.

The horse was hit and floundered. Loosing his stirrups, Brent was thrown free. As he went under the water, something thudded against the side of his head, all but knocking him senseless.

He was aware of bobbing to the surface and then beginning to sink again when a rope slapped against him. Gripping it almost automatically, he hung on as he was pulled through the water. It wasn't until some time later, when he was on solid ground, that he began to piece things together again.

'I thought you were a goner,' Woodcock said, kneeling beside Brent. 'I was too far away to do anything. I guess we've got all the water pumped out of your lungs now.'

'What hit me?' Brent asked.

'Must have been your horse,' Woodcock said. 'He was kicking around, trying to get away from that wagon. I figure one of his hoofs caught you on the side of the noggin. If Rosene hadn't tossed you that rope, I reckon we'd be without a boss now.'

'Rosene?' Brent exclaimed, trying to sit up but dropping back with a groan when it seemed that his head was going to split open.

'She thinks quick and acts just as quick,' Woodcock said. 'She's quite a girl.'

'Any damage to the wagons?' Brent asked.

'One wheel of Hanson's wagon has a busted spoke and felloe. Jake is fixing it now. He should have it fixed by the time you're ready to ride.'

'I'm ready now,' Brent said, but he doubted if even his determination could keep him in the saddle.

A few minutes after Woodcock left, Rosene came by. Brent found himself in an awkard situation. He had never been indebted like this to a girl before.

'I want to thank you for tossing me that rope,' he said finally.

Rosene shrugged. 'I just happened to be close enough to reach you,' she said, and went on about her work with an air that made it plain the matter was closed.

Brent said no more about it, but he couldn't forget it. As Woodcock had said, she was quite a girl.

By noon, Brent was on his feet, but the wagon wheel wasn't repaired yet. Jake had started a fire, dried out the wheel and taken the tire off. He was replacing the broken spoke and felloe. The iron tire would have to be heated now and replaced on the rim, then cooled so it would set.

'We could have used the extra wheel and done this at our night camp,' Brent said when Woodcock came by.

'You weren't going anywhere, anyway,' Woodcock said. 'So I told Jake to fix it while we waited.'

Before the wheel was ready to put back on the wagon, a rider came up from the south. He reined in close to Brent and Woodcock.

'I see you had trouble crossing, too,' he said. 'We're camped down south of here. Took us two days to get all our wagons across and all of today to get patched up so we can move on. I came up to invite you down to our camp for a church service.'

'Have you got a preacher in your train?' Brent asked.

Before the man could answer, Rosene spoke up. 'Pa's down there, isn't he?'

'I don't know who your pa is, miss,' the man said. 'But a man did ride in a little while ago and offered to hold a service for us. He suggested that somebody ride up here and invite you people down.'

Brent sighed. He had promised Dan Hanson that he could hold a short service once they got across the river. He hadn't planned to include another train, but Hanson had already committed himself. Maybe Brent ought to go to the meeting. Certainly he had something to be thankful for after his close brush with death in the river.

'Some of us will be down,' he said.

Brent checked with the men and found that both Jake and Dickie wanted to go to the meeting. Redmond and Voss and Morrie didn't show much interest, so Brent assigned them to watch the herd while the others, including Rosene and her mother, went down to the wagon camp. Rosene drove her wagon while the men rode horses.

When Brent mounted, he discovered that it was about all he could do to stay in the saddle. He decided that maybe it was just as well that they didn't try to move the herd any farther today.

The service convinced Brent that Dan Hanson was really a dedicated man of God. Brent wasn't convinced, however, about the two men who had ridden into his camp with Hanson.

The service wasn't quite over when Brent first noticed the gray horse at the far side of the camp. He promptly forgot what Hanson was saying. A gray horse wasn't unusual among the emigrants, but their horses were draft animals meant to pull wagons and plows. This gray was a long-legged horse meant for a saddle.

Brent nudged Woodcock and pointed to

the horse. Woodcock merely nodded and turned his attention back to Hanson. That was for Rosene's benefit, Brent was sure. She was sitting next to Woodcock on the tongue of a wagon.

Brent eased back out of the crowd. Looking around for Jake and Dickie to help him corner the man with the gray horse, he discovered that the two men were gone. They had been there only a short time ago.

Easing in behind the wagon, Brent began moving around the camp toward the gray horse. By the time he got around the camp, however, the gray horse was gone. Looking toward the river, he saw the rider splashing out into the water. It looked like Oker Patzel, but as sure as Brent was that the owner of the gray horse was Patzel, any rider would look like him at that distance.

By the time Brent got back to his place, Hanson had completed his sermon and was leading everyone in a familiar hymn.

'Have you seen Jake and Dickie?' Brent asked Woodcock as soon as the song was ended.

Woodcock looked around. 'Sure,' he said. 'They're right over there.' He pointed across the crowd.

'They were right here with us when Hanson started talking,' Brent said. 'I'm sure that was Patzel with the gray horse. Maybe Jake and Dickie went over to see him.'

'Aw, you're getting jumpy,' Woodcock said. 'You'd suspect your own mother of double-crossing you.'

'Were you watching them all the time?' Brent demanded.

'Well, no,' Woodcock admitted. 'I had something better to do.'

Brent frowned. Woodcock's eyes had seldom left Rosene except when he was watching her father, and Brent was convinced he had watched Dan Hanson just to impress Rosene with his interest.

'Go tag along with Rosene,' Brent said disgustedly. 'I'm going to find the wagon boss and see if that horse and rider belong to this train.'

Brent wheeled away, but he was aware that Woodcock was tagging along right behind him. Brent had seen the leader of this train when he had introduced Dan Hanson to the crowd, so now he had no trouble picking him out.

'Do you have a man in your train who rides a long-legged gray horse?' Brent asked when he reached him.

The man frowned as he looked over his wagons. 'No, I don't think so. Most of the families have a saddle horse with them, but I don't recall any of them being gray.'

Brent nodded and turned to Woodcock. 'Sounds to me like he was a visitor here today, too.'

'It was probably Patzel,' Woodcock said. 'But I doubt if Jake or Dickie contacted him.'

'Maybe not,' Brent admitted, thinking that he had very little on which to base his suspicions. Nevertheless, they refused to go away. 'We know that Patzel is keeping up with us, anyway. When he thinks the time is right, he'll give us plenty of trouble.'

'I'll agree with that,' Woodcock said, nodding. 'He isn't trailing us for nothing.'

CHAPTER SIX

For a few days the horse herd moved rapidly up the Little Blue, and Brent enjoyed the luck that seemed to be with him. He didn't relax, however. He was positive that Oker Patzel was close by, and that meant that trouble wasn't far away, either.

When they reached the headwaters of the Little Blue, Brent pointed the herd toward the Platte. Fort Kearny was close now. That would mean a rest for the men and a shopping spree for the women in the sutler's store there, although they couldn't buy much.

Brent deliberately hit the Platte River below the fort a few miles. Watering the horses there, he made camp, telling the crew they would move on to the fort first thing in the morning.

It was mid-morning when they came in sight of the cluster of buildings that made up Fort Kearny. Brent suggested that they get an early dinner before riding in to the fort. He assigned Al Redmond, Kyle Voss and Woodcock to stay with the herd while the rest went to the fort. Woodcock complained, but Brent grinned.

'The only pretty girls you'll find here will have red faces. Anyway, I think either you or I should be with the herd all the time. I'm taking Morrie in for some supplies if we can get them. When we get back, you and the other boys can go in.'

'How about taking Ma and me with you?' Rosene asked. 'Looks like a sutler's store there.'

Brent grinned. 'I figured on that. How about you, Dan?'

'I think I'll stay with the wagons,' Dan Hanson said. 'If Jake and Dickie go to the fort, there'll be nobody to keep an eye on the wagons. See over there?'

Brent had already seen the cluster of Indian lodges to the west of the fort. They had been there when he and Morrie had ridden through, going to Westport Landing.

'We'll take one wagon in with us,' Brent said. 'But the one with all our gear in it will be here. You can keep an eye on it. Maybe you'll want to go over to the fort later.'

'You watch the women while you're over

there,' Hanson said.

Brent nodded. 'I'll do that. We're all going to the sutler's store.'

As soon as the meal was over, they started for the fort, leaving Dan Hanson to wash up the dishes. Rosene and her mother rode in the wagon with Morrie, while Brent and Jake and Dickie rode beside the wagon. Morrie turned the wagon toward the sutler's store, and Brent followed, but Jake and Dickie headed for the cluster of buildings that made up the fort.

The store didn't have much variety, but it was better than Brent had really expected, considering how far everything had to be freighted in. Rosene and her mother began fingering some of the bolts of cloth, while Brent turned to the sutler with his list of needed supplies.

'I suppose you get a lot of business from the trails,' Brent said.

'Quite a bit,' the sutler said. 'I set things up here to sell to the soldiers, but the travelers are my best customers now. Do a lot of trading with the Indians, too.'

'Did a fellow on a long-legged gray horse stop in here in the last day or two?'

The sutler rubbed his chin thoughtfully. 'Come to think of it, there was a fellow on a gray horse stopped here yesterday. Friend of yours?'

'I know him,' Brent said. 'Did he say

where he was going?'

'Not that I recall. He just bought some smoking tobacco and jerky. He did ask if the Indians west of here were friendly.'

Brent nodded. 'What did you tell him?'

'They're friendly, all right. In fact, they're friendly enough to steal the shirt right off your back.'

Brent's attention was pulled to the door as it was darkened by a huge man who stood there, looking over the interior of the store. Brent couldn't see him very well until he stepped inside where the light wasn't forming a halo around him.

He looked to Brent as big as Jake Closter. He was dirtier than Jake; even his beard was matted to his chin by some sticky substance, probably syrup from his morning pancakes. His shirt didn't look as if it had ever seen water other than sweat. Brent almost imagined he could smell him all the way across the room.

The sutler stepped over to some Indians who were standing next to the tobacco case, and Brent waited for him to come back and fill the list he and Morrie had made out.

Morrie had gone over to the corner to look at a buckskin jacket, and Brent was watching him when he heard a rough laugh and turned to see the big dirty man crowding in between Rosene and her mother. His attention was on Rosene, and there was nothing gentle or subtle about the gleam in his eyes.

Brent frowned. Rosene had let him know that she could take care of herself but he wasn't sure she could this time. If he interfered, however, she'd probably take him to task for it.

'I heard there was a pretty girl over here at the store,' the big man said in a voice that matched his size.

He reached out a hand to touch Rosene, but she jerked away, giving him a withering look. He only laughed and stabbed a hand out to grab her arm. Rosene tried to pull away, but he just laughed louder and tightened his grip on her arm. Mrs. Hanson grabbed the man from the other side and tried to pull him away from Rosene.

The man wheeled part way toward Mrs. Hanson and gave her the back of his free hand, sending her reeling. Brent started across the store in long strides. Before he got there, however, Emily Hanson had jerked the long pin out of her hat and made a dive at the big man. He screamed like a wounded panther when she jabbed the pin into his rump.

The man released his hold on Rosene and wheeled on Mrs. Hanson. But Brent was there by then, and he caught the man's arm and whirled him around.

The sutler screamed, 'Get out of here! Fight outside!'

The big man was breathing hard with fury. 'That's fine with me.' He almost ran out the door.

Brent followed him outside, knowing that if he didn't go out, the man would come back in after him. He saw a half-dozen men gathered at the corner of the building. Jake and Dickie Closter were there, and it struck Brent that they must have told the man about Rosene being at the store.

Then he realized that it hadn't been Rosene the man had really come for. It had been Brent. He was as sure of that as he was that he was in for the fight of his life.

CHAPTER SEVEN

Brent realized that the man was a good fighter when he squared around to face him once they were outside the sutler's store. He showed both caution and poise. Brent wondered if he had been waiting at the fort for him and had found out from Jake and Dickie that he was at the store. That seemed reasonable, especially since the sutler had said that the man on the gray horse had been there yesterday.

The giant waited until Brent was out in the beaten-down area in front of the store, then charged at him. There was nothing scientific about the way the big man came at Brent, yet he kept up his guard. Brent's only defense was to get out of the way, because he could see the raw power there. If the man ever got Brent in his arms, he'd crush him like an eggshell.

Brent tried to hit the man as the force of his charge carried him past, but the man was quick and wheeled around, almost catching Brent before he could leap away again.

Brent got in a few blows in those first exchanges, but they didn't land solidly and only irritated the giant. In return, Brent was receiving some good jolts, their force testifying to the strength of the man.

Brent was rocked particularly hard by one blow, and as he reeled backward, he saw the giant coming at him, disregarding caution as he tried to take advantage of Brent's retreat. Rallying himself, Brent suddenly drove forward, surprising the big man and slamming both fists into his face with all the power he could muster. One blow split the man's lip, and blood trickled down into his beard.

He didn't lose his balance or his ability to defend himself, however, and Brent held back, watching for another opening before driving in again. Respect showed in the giant's face as he circled Brent. His reckless charges were replaced by short drives, with one fist jabbing while the other guarded his face. The man knew the art of self-defense, Brent realized. Somehow Brent had to bring him out from behind that defense if he expected to stay on even terms in the battle.

For a while, the fight became a stand-off, neither man willing to risk a charge unless he saw a good opening. Brent had decided the man was a slow thinker so, after taking a light jab, he backed off hastily, hoping to draw the man into a reckless charge.

A triumphant gleam came into the man's eyes as Brent retreated, and he dropped his cautious boxing and drove forward. Brent dodged to his right and slammed a fist against the big man's ear as he stumbled, trying to check himself.

The man, already off balance, went down. Swearing coarsely, he rolled over, digging a gun out of his waistband. Brent hadn't brought his gun, not expecting any trouble at the fort. He was too far from the big man to reach him before he could squeeze the trigger.

As the man jerked the gun up, however, a long whip lashed out and wrapped itself around his wrist, snapping the gun away into the dust. Brent shot a glance around to see Morrie Zimmerman standing by his wagon, where he had evidently been waiting, the whip in his hand, debating about getting into the fight.

The big man was scrambling to his feet,

and Brent turned his attention back to him. Lunging forward, he caught the man before he got quite balanced and slammed a hard fist into his face, sending him sprawling again. The man tried to get up again, and once more Brent flattened him. Fury drove Brent as he thought of the man pulling a gun when Brent was obviously unarmed. He wasn't plagued by any sense of unfairness as he repeatedly slammed the man down before he could get to his feet.

The man was strong and stubborn. Three more times he tried to get up, but each time Brent knocked him down before he could quite make it. After the last try, he lay there and glared up at Brent.

'Had enough?' Brent demanded.

The man got to his knees. 'There'll be another time,' he muttered.

'If you still want to fight, we'll finish it now,' Brent said, and stepped forward, hitting him in the face with all the strength he had left.

The man rolled backward and flopped over on his back, his eyes glazed. Brent stood over him, waiting for him to move.

'That's enough, boss,' Jake Closter said. 'You blamed near killed him.'

'I wouldn't cry if I had,' Brent panted.

He turned back into the store, where Rosene and her mother were watching.

'You did try to kill him, didn't you?'

Rosene said accusingly.

Brent was too tired and hurt in too many places to care what Rosene thought. 'I would have if he'd kept asking for it. Get the things you want. We're heading back to camp as soon as we get our supplies.'

As they loaded their purchases into the wagon, Morrie said, 'Seems funny that fellow would be so anxious to fight. I don't believe he was that struck with Rosene.'

'He was after me,' Brent said. 'I know Patzel hired him. Maybe that was why I wanted to kill him.'

'You did show your ornery side to Rosene and her mother,' Morrie said.

Brent snorted. 'What do I care about that?'

'Do you think Patzel will try to steal the herd now?' Morrie asked after a while.

'I doubt it,' Brent said. 'He might have if that giant had managed to kill me. But Patzel is in no hurry. We're taking the horses in the same direction he'd take them if he had the herd.'

Brent and Morrie brought the last of their purchases out of the store and found three Indians standing by the horses admiring them. Brent watched them closely as he took his load to the wagon.

'Good horse,' one Indian said when Brent moved over to them.

'Fair,' Brent said.

The Indian shook his head. 'Good horse,'

he repeated. 'Plenty good.'

The three Indians walked around the team, touching the horses almost reverently. Rosene and her mother started to leave the store but backed out of sight when they saw the Indians. After another turn around the horses, the Indians said something to each other, then nodded and went back toward the fort.

'What did they want?' Rosene asked when she came out of the store after the Indians were gone.

'These horses, I reckon,' Brent said.

'Better watch them redskins,' the sutler warned from the doorway. 'They'll steal anything that isn't fastened down.'

'They'll get something they didn't ask for if they try to steal our horses,' Morrie said bravely.

'How many Indians are around the fort?' Brent asked.

'Hard to say, the way they come and go,' the sutler replied. 'I'd guess there's maybe a dozen young bucks like you just saw. They're the ones you have to watch out for. The older ones ain't liable to bother you.'

'Don't they know what will happen to them if they steal a horse?' Morrie demanded.

'They think that stealing horses is a show of great courage,' the sutler said. 'It's something like counting coup. A man who counts coup or steals horses from an enemy becomes a mighty warrior in his tribe. Good horses like you've got would be a real prize, too.'

'We'll watch out for them,' Brent said. 'Let's go, Morrie.'

Morrie backed the team around and headed for the camp south of the fort. Brent resolved to keep a heavy guard around the herd while they were this close to the fort.

As always, the dogs were a big help during the dark hours of the night. Twice they barked at something on the fringes of the herd.

The women had breakfast ready at dawn, and by sunup the herd was moving out. Throughout the day Brent kept a sharp watch for Indians, but he saw none and began to relax a little. However, he put three men on guard around the herd, and he kept both dogs with them. The night passed uneventfully, and Brent allowed himself to hope that the Indians had stayed at the fort.

The second day out, however, he sighted an Indian on the hills to the south. He called Woodcock's attention to the rider, and Woodcock alerted the rest of the men.

'Think they'll attack?' Morrie asked anxiously as they started to make camp for the night.

'I doubt it,' Brent said. 'The one we saw was just a scout, but I have a hunch the only ones with him are the young bucks from the fort. They're far enough away now so that the soldiers can't interfere if they want to steal a few horses. According to the sutler, there are only a few of them.'

'They may have picked up a hundred friends by now,' Woodcock put in.

'That's possible,' Brent admitted, 'but not likely. We'll keep a heavy guard on the herd. The dogs will warn us if anybody gets close.'

'I don't know how we'd have made out without those dogs,' Morrie said.

'We'd have been in worse trouble than we are,' Brent admitted. 'We'd better not let the horses spread out too much tonight. Those Indians may try to stampede them.'

'These horses won't stampede as easily as some,' Woodcock said. 'They're too gentle.'

Brent sent Woodcock, Jake Closter and Kyle Voss out to the herd right after supper. He expected everyone else to get to bed as quickly as possible, because the men were going to have to take their turns with the herd before the night was over. However, Al Redmond, who loved to play cards, coaxed Dickie Closter into a few hands of poker before they turned in.

Brent thought little of it until he heard the two men arguing violently. He rolled out of his blankets just in time to see Redmond leap up, grabbing for a knife that he carried in a sheath at his waist.

Dickie's hand moved with unbelievable

speed, whipping out his gun. He didn't shoot, but brought the gun around in an arc and slammed the barrel against the side of Redmond's head. Redmond slumped forward and sprawled in the grass.

Dickie stared down at Redmond for a moment, then holstered his gun, picked up the money and went back to the spot where he had left his bedroll.

Brent had been too far away to interfere. Now he moved toward Redmond, wondering how badly he was hurt. He couldn't forget the speed of Dickie's draw. Redmond had actually moved fast, yet Dickie had drawn his gun and slammed it against Redmond's head before Redmond could do any damage with his knife.

Brent reached Redmond and knelt beside him. Redmond was beginning to stir, apparently only momentarily stunned. Brent helped him sit up.

'What was the argument about?' Brent asked.

Redmond felt his head gingerly. 'He was cheating, and I called him. He nearly busted my head open.'

'You'd better be more careful who you pick to play cards with,' Brent said.

'I'm going to bust his head open just like he did mine!' Redmond snapped.

'I'd think twice before I tried that, too,' Brent warned. 'He's plenty fast with that gun. He could have killed you just as easily as he parted your hair.'

'I reckon so,' Redmond growled, getting to his feet and staggering over to his bedroll.

Redmond would be no good on guard duty tonight, Brent thought. He'd go out himself with Dickie and Morrie when it came time to relieve the three men already there.

Sunup found Redmond with a big headache but able to ride and do his share of the work. There had been no sign of Indians during the night, but Brent took no encouragement from that. He knew they were still out there.

As if to verify his suspicions, he saw two of them about mid-forenoon, sitting on their ponies on a hill off to the south, watching the herd. Woodcock rode up beside Brent, his eyes on the Indians, too.

'I was hoping they had given up,' he said.

'They won't until they've had a try at getting some of these horses.'

'What are they waiting for?'

'Could be they're picking their own time and place,' Brent said. 'Or maybe they've sent for help. Might take quite a while to find their hunting parties.'

A few minutes later, Dan Hanson rode one of his old horses over to Brent. Brent looked from him to the wagon he was supposed to be driving. His wife had the reins, and Brent decided they were in as good hands as they had been when Dan Hanson had been driving.

'Where do you think they're going?' Brent asked, bringing his attention back to Dan on his bony old horse.

'I saw those Indians, too,' Hanson said. 'They're going to give us trouble unless we act first.'

'What do you propose doing?'

'The only humane thing,' Hanson said. 'Hold out the hand of peace. I intend to ride out there and invite them into camp, where we can share some food with them and let them know that we mean no harm.'

'They already know that,' Brent said disgustedly, amazed at Hanson's reasoning. 'If there is any harm meant, it's the other way around.'

'If I can only get a chance to talk to them, I can convince them of the brotherhood of man, regardless of the color of his skin,' Hanson said.

'It's not the color of our skins that interests those Indians,' Brent said. 'It's these horses. All the talking you can do wouldn't change their minds a bit about stealing them.'

'Do you mean you won't let me ride out there?'

'That's exactly what I mean,' Brent said forcefully. 'If they didn't kill you, they'd at least put you afoot, although I doubt if they'd want that horse.'

'I think we should reason with them,' Hanson said, disappointment in his face.

'We'll reason with them, all right, if they come close to camp,' Brent said. 'But we'll pick a type of reasoning they'll understand, which isn't likely to be words.'

Hanson rode slowly back to his wagon, while Brent turned his attention to the herd, wondering what he could do to discourage the Indians from making a raid on the horses.

The grass was good close to the river when they watered the herd before going into camp, so Brent decided to camp on the spot. It would save a drive to the river in the morning to water the horses before starting out on the trail.

Brent put Redmond and Dickie on different hours of guard duty. After last night's argument over the card game, he didn't trust them together. Brent rode out to be with the herd as dusk settled down. If the Indians struck, he expected it to be at dusk or dawn. He'd be out again at dawn.

There was a stiff breeze blowing in from the south-west toward the river. The dogs were restless, stopping often to sniff the wind and growl.

'They smell those redskins,' Redmond said once when he met Brent slowly circling the herd. 'They're out there, and they're up to something.'

'The wind's getting pretty strong,' Brent

said. 'They could move in close, and we wouldn't hear them.'

Redmond nodded. 'I'm guessing that's what they're doing. And the dogs smell them.'

Brent was about ready to go back to camp when he saw a flicker of light off to the southwest. He reined up and stared at it. Then he discovered another flicker almost directly to the south. A moment later another flash of light cut through the darkness to the west.

The Indians were up to something. As the lights rapidly flared up brighter and began to spread, lighting the sky with their glow, he realized what it was. Wheeling his horse, he rode to the wagons only a short distance away.

'Fire!' he yelled.

As the sleepers rolled out of their blankets, he pointed to the flames, now reaching out hungrily toward each other to form a quarter-circle of fire sweeping toward the river. He understood the Indians' strategy. Normally, they wouldn't set fire to the grass the buffalo needed, but this fire wouldn't burn far. The wind was sweeping it directly toward the river, where it would go out.

Between the fire and the river, however, were Brent's camp and the horse herd. The camp would be destroyed and the horses scattered. The Indians could take their time gathering up the loose horses.

CHAPTER EIGHT

'Hitch up the teams!' Brent shouted.

The four horses to be used on the wagons the next day were picketed close by so that no time would be lost in rounding them up at daylight. Brent swung off his horse and pulled the picket pins on one team while Morrie ran for the other. By the time they got the horses to the wagons, the camp was exploding into frenzied activity.

'Where will we go?' Hanson shouted.

'Only one way we can go,' Brent yelled. 'Into the river.'

After supper Rosene and her mother had left much of their cooking equipment outside the wagons, ready to use for breakfast. Now they were tossing it wildly into the wagon.

'We can't cross the river in the dark,' Hanson complained.

'Would you rather burn right here?' Brent said, not even looking at the missionary.

Redmond came to help Brent and Morrie slap the harness on the horses.

'That fire is coming fast,' he said. 'What about the herd?'

'Our only chance is to push the horses across the river, too,' Brent said. 'Where's

Woodcock?'

'He and Jake and Dickie are out with the herd. Voss is probably there, too.'

'Good. Go tell them to start the horses across. I'll be along as soon as I get these wagons moving.'

Brent finished harnessing his team, then stepped one horse across the tongue of the wagon, running to the front to hook up the neck yoke. He glanced at the fire, gaining momentum with alarming speed. The Indians had tested the wind well. The center of the fire was aimed directly at the camp.

Brent wondered if the horses would go into the river at night. If they didn't, they would scatter along the south bank of the river. He doubted if any of them would be caught by the fire; but after the fire had burned itself out, the Indians would have no trouble picking up as many horses as they wanted.

Brent hooked the last tug on his team, then ran over to help Morrie. He heard the horses running toward the river. Either the fire or the crew had started them.

'Morrie, you take this wagon with Mrs. Hanson,' Brent shouted. 'Rosene, you and your father take the other wagon. Head for that island we saw when we camped tonight. It's not too far from shore. You should be safe from the fire there. It's too dangerous to try to go all the way across the river.'

Morrie leaped into the front of one wagon

and slapped the lines, shouting to the Morgans. They hit the collars with a snap, excited by the fire and the commotion of the last few minutes. Rosene had the reins in the other wagon, Brent saw. He was glad of that. Dan Hanson would probably manage to upset the wagon somehow if he was driving.

Brent wheeled his horse to the west, where he could crowd the leaders of the running herd downstream away from the wagons. If they went into the water above the wagons, some swimming horse would be almost sure to flounder into a team and wagon. There'd be enough accidents without deliberately setting the stage for one.

He met a rider as he was pushing the horses downstream. Recognizing Woodcock, he shouted, 'Get all the horses?'

Woodcock nodded. 'They stick together pretty well. We'd better have them running hard when they hit the water. Don't give them a chance to balk.'

'Right,' Brent shouted. 'Keep them downstream from the wagons.'

Seeing that the herd was running well, he swung back upstream to check on the wagons. Both Morrie and Rosene had their teams in the water now. The light from the fire was making weird dancing shadows over the area, lighting the landscape enough so that Brent could see that the wagons were heading straight for the little island, only a short distance away.

Assured that the wagons were on their way to safety, Brent wheeled back to the horse herd. Even in the heavy grass, the hundred horses were stirring up some dust. That, mingled with the smoke from the fire that was now rolling over the area, made it difficult to tell for sure that all the horses were in the herd bearing down on the river.

Riding to the southwest, Brent circled behind the horses. He had no fear of the Indians now. They would wait until the fire had burned itself out; then they would come along the river to pick up the scattered horses. Brent intended to make sure they found nothing.

Heat pressed down on Brent, and suddenly he heard nothing but the roar of the fire. The horses had all swept past him toward the river.

Reining around, Brent dug in his spurs and raced after them. By the time he reached the river bank, he saw that all the herd was in the water. The river was wide, but in very few places was it belly deep on a horse. For the most part, the horses were sloshing through the water and sand, making a terrific commotion and noise.

Brent turned in the saddle for one last sweep of the burning grass. He didn't see a thing there. If any horse had fallen behind, he was in that fire now.

Kicking his horse forward, he plunged into the river, too. By the flickering light of the fire, he saw other riders urging the horses across to the far bank. They were halfway across when Brent became aware that some of the horses were drifting downstream.

He reined his horse to his right to get below them. The herd had to be kept together. If the horses were allowed to drift apart before they got out of the river, they would scatter, and the Indians could pick them up on the north bank as well as the south.

'Keep them bunched!' Brent shouted, swinging his rope at the head of a sleek bay that insisted on going downstream.

Watching the men work, Brent felt a pride in his crew. They had recognized the danger in letting the horses scatter and were working hard to keep them together. There were men in the crew that Brent didn't fully trust, but they were doing their job now.

Suddenly Brent's attention was caught by a rider to his left whose horse had stopped short, throwing him almost out of the saddle. The horse was floundering around now, and Brent knew that he was in quicksand. The river had many quicksand bars, and this sand had just been stirred by the passing herd and was more unstable than usual. The horse had apparently tried to make a sharp turn in the sand, and his feet had dug in so deep that he couldn't pull them out.

Brent reined toward the rider as he saw him thrown sideways out of the saddle into the water and sand. The water wasn't deep enough here to drown a man unless he lay down in it. But it was the shallowest water that harbored the most treacherous quicksand.

As Brent rode closer, he could see the man struggling as hard as the horse to get out of the sand. The horse was floundering over toward the rider and in a minute could crash into him.

Brent flipped out his rope. It was wet and stiff, but he could still throw it where he wanted it to go.

'Catch this,' he shouted.

Brent wasn't sure the man heard him, but he threw the rope, anyway. Just as the rope hit the man, the horse made a mighty lunge and came down almost on him.

'Got it?' Brent shouted, but there was no answer.

He tugged on the rope and felt it tighten. Either the man had the rope, or it was caught under the horse. Brent turned his horse and nudged him away from the quicksand. The rope remained taut, and in a moment, the man slid away from the horse. Brent reined back toward the fallen rider. The horse, in the meantime, had struggled out of the sand and was trotting toward the north bank of the river, snorting the water and sand out of his nostrils.

'That sure happened fast,' Al Redmond said as Brent reached him and held a hand down to lift him up behind his saddle. 'Thought sure I was a goner.'

'Doesn't look like a little quicksand bar could cause so much trouble,' Brent said.

Redmond climbed up behind Brent and put his arms around Brent's waist. 'That old horse came right down on me. If I hadn't had that rope, I reckon I'd be bloated up on creek water now.'

Brent turned his horse toward the north bank. He recognized Redmond's words for what they were intended to be: thanks for saving his life. He'd say no more about it, and he knew Redmond wouldn't, either.

The horses were out of the river now, and Brent could see the men driving the ones who had come out too far downstream up the river bank toward the main herd.

Woodcock pushed some horses past them, then reined up. He took a look at Redmond and whistled softly.

'Holy smoke! Don't you know this is no time to take a swim?'

Redmond spat disgustedly. 'No time to buy a ticket to the happy hunting ground, either, but I almost had one.'

Brent stared across the river at the fire, eating its way down close to the water now. 'Seen anything of the Indians who started that fire?'

'Haven't been looking,' Woodcock said. 'We had our hands full with these horses. Don't think we lost any.'

'Will those wagons be safe that close to the other side?' Redmond asked.

'Been asking myself the same thing,' Brent said. 'Feel like going back with me to make sure?'

'Sure do,' Redmond said. 'Catch my horse for me, Woodie. And give me a dry gun.' He slid off Brent's horse.

'Watch the herd,' Brent called to Woodcock. 'Those Indians may decide to cross over and try to take the herd, anyway.'

'They'll get a hot reception if they do,' Woodcock promised.

He gave Redmond his gun, then wheeled away to catch his horse. Brent turned back to the river and waited till Redmond caught up.

Across the river, on the hill behind the fire, Brent could see some moving figures through the smoke. He pointed toward them, and Redmond nodded.

'Moving in to pick up the spoils,' Redmond said.

'Except that there isn't going to be anything to pick up. They'll be plenty mad, and those wagons may look pretty inviting to them.'

'Reckon they will, with only an old man, a kid and two women to defend them.'

Brent kicked his horse into the river. Redmond, still wet from his dunking a few minutes earlier, followed him. Brent wondered if he should have left Redmond to help guard the horse herd and brought Woodcock. But if it came to a battle with guns, he'd rather have Redmond's gun beside him than the Englishman's.

The fire was dwindling fast now as it reached the water's edge and sputtered out for a lack of fuel. With the fire dying away, the light in the area faded, too. But there was still enough light from the last flickering fingers of flame to reveal the Indians coming down gingerly over the burned area.

'They ain't even waiting for all the fire to go out,' Redmond said, nudging his horse to a splashing trot through the water.

'They'll probably back off when they find out what the situation is,' Brent said.

But he urged his horse to a faster trot, too. From the south bank, it had seemed like quite a way out to the island where he had directed the wagons. But coming back to the island from the north, it appeared that the island was very close to the south bank.

The Indians were having trouble with their horses as the ponies tried to get off the hot ground. They soon reined back to the top of the hill, but Brent was sure it wasn't until they saw that every sign of the camp was gone.

Brent and Redmond reached the island and found the two wagons with the teams still hitched and Morrie giving directions to Dan Hanson and Rosene on how to guide the wagons the rest of the way across the river.

'You're not figuring on trying to go on across, are you?' Brent demanded.

'I sure ain't fixing to stay here and try to fight off that bunch of redskins,' Morrie said. 'They can get too close even if they don't come out into the water. Of course, I wasn't figuring on you coming back to help us.'

'We're not about to leave you over here alone.'

'Especially since you have all our grub,' Redmond added with a grin.

The island was small, only about fifty feet long and no more than forty feet wide. Brent stationed Rosene at the west end to watch upstream for any Indians who might try to get out in the river and come down on the island from above. He put Mrs. Hanson at the lower end of the island with the same instructions. Then he placed Dan Hanson and Morrie between himself and Redmond under the wagons, facing the river bank.

He had barely settled himself when the Indians began moving down off the hill again. The ground had cooled fast, because the fire hadn't burned long.

The Indians kicked their horses into a gallop as soon as they were off the hills. It was so dark that Brent could barely see them. But he could hear them distinctly.

At the water's edge, they stopped. They had surely seen the horse herd cross the river or had guessed what had happened. They had also seen the wagons on the island. There were a few rifles among the Indians, and those rifles roared now, the bullets slapping into the water. Only one hit a wagon.

'Not very good shots,' Redmond muttered, and fired his rifle.

'Better hold your fire till you can see what you're aiming at,' Brent suggested.

'Think they'll charge us?' Hanson asked nervously.

'I doubt it,' Brent said. 'They wouldn't have stopped and wasted those shots if they'd planned to rush us. It was the horses they wanted, not us.'

The Indians fired a few more shots in the general direction of the island, then rode down the river.

'I'd better get back to the horses,' Redmond said after everything was quiet. 'They might cross the river and make a try at them.'

Brent agreed. 'I'll stay with the wagons just in case they come back. If you get in trouble, I'll come over and help.'

Redmond rode away, and those on the island settled down for the night, Brent and Morrie taking turns keeping watch.

The night passed quietly, and at the first streaks of dawn, Brent peered through the growing light at the north bank. The horse herd was there, some of the animals up and grazing.

Brent rode his horse to the south bank and over the burned area to the top of the hill. There were no Indians in sight. Coming back to the island, he helped get the wagons to the south bank. There Rosene and her mother got breakfast, while Brent rode across the river to the men with the herd. They took turns crossing to eat, and it was mid-forenoon before Brent was ready to cross the herd.

In daylight, pushing the herd across the river was no problem, except that some of the animals didn't want to go into the water. Last night they hadn't hesitated, with the fire directly behind them.

Twice in the crossing, Brent floundered into quicksand that would have stuck a wagon. He realized how fortunate they had been to find an island close to the south bank where the wagons could escape the fire. Only a miracle could have gotten them all the way across the river safely in the dark.

After a late dinner, Brent got the herd moving again, but they went only a short distance to a spot where the grass was good.

Brent placed a heavy guard around the herd, using both dogs, but the night passed without any alarm. As soon as breakfast was over the next morning, Brent got the herd moving, then took his Morgan and rode ahead.

He was convinced that the little band of Indians who had tried to scatter the herd with the fire the other night were the Indians from Fort Kearny, and he surmised that they had given up and gone back to the fort where they could get what they needed without any work. But there was a chance that they were still hanging around, waiting for another opportunity to try to get the herd. He had to find out.

Leaving Woodcock in charge of the herd, Brent pushed ahead along the river. He lost track of time until the sun was almost overhead. He didn't know how far ahead of the herd he was, but he hadn't seen any Indians and he was convinced that those who had tried to burn the camp the other night had gone back to the fort.

He stopped on a hilltop to scan the country again before turning back. As he reined around to start back to the herd, he caught his breath. On a hilltop that he had passed only a few minutes before were three Indians, and they were watching him intently.

Brent sat motionless for a minute. He'd have to go past the Indians to get back to the herd. Three Indians would never let one white man get away with a horse like the Morgan Brent was riding. On the other hand, if he rode forward, he'd be getting farther from help. Brent had no illusions that he could handle three Indians in a battle.

His decision was suddenly made for him. The three Indians apparently had convinced themselves that Brent was alone, and they kicked their horses into a run toward him.

Brent reined to the south. It gave the Indians an angle on him, but he had to get around them to make it back to the herd. He knew his chances weren't good.

CHAPTER NINE

Brent let the Morgan stretch out and show his speed for the first half-mile. He couldn't allow the Indians to get too close. He had to circle his pursuers, and every time he reined closer to the direction he wanted to go, he gave the Indians a better angle than before.

Brent was amazed at the speed of the Morgan. In a straight-away race, it would have been no contest with the Indians. But each time he gained a little ground, he angled more toward the east. The farther south he went, the longer the run would be back to the herd.

The fact that the Indians couldn't catch Brent only seemed to intensify their determination to get his horse. They obviously realized where Brent was trying to go.

Brent saw that one Indian had dropped off the chase and was cutting back to the river. He'd head down the river and wait for Brent as he circled around. He'd have a fresher horse then to take up the chase.

When the Indians began to slow down, Brent reined his Morgan up a little. Even from that distance, he could see that the Indians' ponies were about done in. Brent's Morgan was puffing heavily, but he was far from finished.

At the slower pace set now by the Indians, Brent gradually pulled away from his pursuers and reined his horse more toward the river, finally hitting an angle that he thought would bring him to the herd. The Indian horses behind him were too tired now to take advantage of the angle Brent was pursuing.

Brent's Morgan was lathered at the withers and around the edge of the saddle blanket, but Brent had seen only a few flecks of foam from his mouth. He showed no sign yet of giving out.

Once he had settled on a straight course toward the river, Brent began to pull away from his pursuers. They had lost the race, and they had to know it. Yet they kept on his trail. If they gave up, Brent would stop and rest his horse and be ready for the other

Indian when he jumped him. They weren't going to give Brent a chance to do that.

He reined back to a long trot. The Indians behind tried to kick their horses to a faster speed, but speed just wasn't in the little ponies any more.

For half a mile, Brent held his horse to a trot. Then, seeing that the Indians were gaining on him again, he shook the reins, and the Morgan willingly increased his speed. He soon left the Indians behind.

Just as Brent began looking for a break in the rolling hills that would lead down to the river, the other Indian appeared almost directly between him and the river. He was going to have to outrun this Indian, too, and go around him.

This young buck was on a fresher horse than those behind Brent, but his pony showed the effects of his run down the river to cut Brent off from the herd. However, this was not going to be an even race. Brent's Morgan had been pushed steadily now for more than half an hour.

Yet when Brent shook the reins, the Morgan responded with another show of speed that kept a respectable distance between him and his pursuer. Brent held his horse due east for a time, parallel to the river, not giving the Indian any advantage in his pursuit.

He had circled far to the south in going

around the Indians, and he figured that now he must be almost even with the herd. He couldn't afford to go beyond it.

A half-mile later, Brent realized that the Indian was not going to be able to shorten the distance between him and the Morgan. In open challenge, Brent reined the Morgan to the northeast toward the river trail, allowing the Indian a better angle in his pursuit.

The Indian kicked his horse into a supreme effort, but he had no chance. Brent held his horse to a steady pace and cut into a long gully that dropped down to the river. Seeing that it was hopeless, the Indian threw up the rifle he was carrying and fired a shot after Brent. The shot missed, and Brent breathed easier. The chase was over. The Indian wouldn't have fired that shot at the horse if he'd had any hope of owning it.

Brent reached the level of the river bottom and almost bumped into two riders charging into the mouth of the canyon. They reined up sharply.

'Who's shooting?' Woodcock demanded.

Brent patted the steaming neck of his horse, feeling elation pouring through him. He had admired the Morgans before. But only now did he really appreciate their stamina and speed.

'A disgusted buck,' he said. 'Three of them tried to run down this horse. But we could have outrun the whole Sioux nation.'

Woodcock grinned. 'I told you these Morgans were good horses.'

'Nobody could have made me believe how good till I saw it with my own eyes,' Brent said.

'Just three Indians?' Jake Closter asked nervously.

'That's all,' Brent said. 'And they're on horses that are practically dead now. If there had been more Indians around, they'd have gotten in on the chase, too. There's nothing to worry about.'

Brent rode over to the wagons, where Rosene handed him a slice of bread and some meat that she had kept warm from the noon meal stop.

'Can't expect much when you don't come at the right time,' she said.

'I'm lucky to get anything.'

'What happened, Tom?' she asked, concern breaking through her show of irritation.

Brent slapped a hand on the Morgan's neck. 'This horse just showed the Indians what a real runner looks like. I've got to cool him off now and get me another horse to ride the rest of the day.'

Unsaddling the Morgan, he rubbed him down, then tied him to the rear of the wagon where he could walk steadily for half an hour. Then he caught another horse, a black this time, and dropped back to the herd.

Within an hour, everyone in the crew had heard about Brent's chase, and the admiration for the Morgans swelled to personal pride in the drovers. Woodcock beamed with importance, for he had been bragging about the Morgans ever since they had left Westport Landing, but no one had really taken him seriously.

With the feeling that the Indian threat was gone for the time being, the men moved the herd out the next morning with the nearest thing to a carefree attitude they'd had since leaving the Missouri. Rosene turned the reins of her team over to her mother, mounted one of her father's old horses and rode out to the herd. Hanson's old team, which had looked ready to collapse when he'd driven into camp that first night, was now picking up flesh and showing some spirit. Neither horse had been hooked to a wagon since then.

Woodcock dropped off his spot at swing and came back to where Rosene had taken up a position. Within minutes, Kyle Voss had come over from his drag spot to vie with Woodcock for Rosene's attention.

Brent, riding point, glanced back and saw the herd spreading out more than usual, grabbing mouthfuls of grass along the trail. He realized what was wrong and dropped back to the rear of the herd. He couldn't afford any slowdown. The threat of Indians had abated for the moment, but that didn't erase the danger of Oker Patzel. Patzel was waiting his chance, Brent knew, and the longer the herd was on the trail, the more opportunities Patzel would have to strike.

Woodcock and Voss saw Brent coming and hurriedly returned to their posts. Rosene barely looked at Brent as he reined in beside her.

'No need to say it,' she said sharply. 'You think I'm a drawback here. But I love to ride, and I can help.'

'You could help, all right,' Brent said. 'But I don't need three riders pushing along one horse.'

'I didn't ask them to come over.'

Brent was jolted by the sting of her words. He felt ashamed. Rosene wasn't the one he should criticize. Woodcock and Voss were the culprits, but it wouldn't do any good to chastise them.

'I suppose you think I should do my riding away from the herd,' Rosene said when Brent kept quiet.

'Not too far from the herd,' Brent warned.

'If you think I'm going to ride on that bumpy wagon all day, you're crazy,' she flared, and reined her horse around with a jerk.

Brent watched her ride off to the south. At the top of the bluffs south of the river, she rode parallel to the herd like a scout. Brent kept a closer eye on her than he did on the horses. She disappeared over the bluff to the south, and his concern mounted.

When she didn't reappear after twenty minutes, he reined his Morgan toward the hills. He was just climbing to the top of the bluff when she showed up above him.

'Now who's leaving his post with the herd?' she demanded, her eyes twinkling.

'It's not safe for you to be riding out here alone,' he said sharply. 'You should know that.'

'I never got so far from the herd that I couldn't get back before any Indian could catch me.'

'Indians aren't the only danger out here.'

Her face sobered. 'You're thinking of the man on the gray horse?'

Brent nodded. 'And you can be sure he's not alone.'

'I'll stay within sight of the herd,' Rosene promised finally, 'but I'm not going to be a prisoner in that wagon.'

She kicked her old horse in the ribs and sent him down the bluff toward the wagons. Brent swung around and followed her. It was obvious that he'd never be able to hold her down. But on that old horse, she wouldn't have a chance of escaping if she got caught any distance from the herd.

Back with the horses, Brent rode up alongside Woodcock. 'Can you pick out a good gentle horse from the herd for Rosene to ride?' he asked.

Woodcock nodded. 'I sure can.' He grinned at Brent. 'She's getting to you, too, is she?'

Brent scowled at Woodcock. 'What do you mean by that?'

'You're worried about her. You didn't give a hoot what happened to her when she first joined up with us. She's getting to you just like she's getting to every single man on the drive.'

Brent balled his fist. 'Now if you think—'

Woodcock waved a hand in surrender and grinned. 'All right. Just say you're concerned about the safety of everybody on the drive. But I've been around women enough to know when a man begins to fall.'

'Aw, shut up!' Brent snapped. 'You pick out that horse tonight.'

Brent wheeled away to his post on point where Jake Closter had been riding alone. He couldn't get Woodcock's accusations out of his mind. Maybe he was more concerned about Rosene now than he had been. But he had a herd to get through to California. Having Rosene captured or even chased by Indians would throw the drive into a turmoil. Patzel might think of kidnapping her to disrupt the drive. If she was mounted on one of these Morgans, she'd have a much better chance of escaping trouble. Brent didn't fool himself into thinking he could keep her from riding out where danger lurked.

Woodcock presented Rosene with a sleek bay Morgan that night right after supper, and he obviously enjoyed his task. The Englishman was attracted to Rosene, and he wasn't alone. Woodcock had called it right when he'd said all the men were drawn to her, especially Kyle Voss.

Brent couldn't keep his eyes off Woodcock and Voss vying for Rosene's attention as she and her mother did the dishes and got things ready to make breakfast tomorrow morning. When Woodcock came to his blankets, Brent was waiting for him.

'What did she say about the horse?'

'Oh, she was as tickled as a little girl with a new doll,' Woodcock said. 'But if you think I explained that you told me to get her that horse, you're crazy. I'm not passing up a chance like that.'

'I didn't expect you to,' Brent said.

'Of course, she figured it out for herself,' Woodcock admitted. 'She said she wasn't going to ride that horse because you said she had to, but she'd do it if I told her to.'

'So you did?'

'Of course. I don't want her hair decorating some teepee. That wouldn't be much worse, though, than letting that sidewinder, Voss, have her.'

Brent shot a glance at Woodcock. 'Is Voss making any headway with her?'

'To be honest, nobody is. But you might.'

Brent snorted. 'She hates me. She makes that pretty plain. She doesn't like to be bossed. But I'm taking this herd through, and nobody is going to stop me.'

Woodcock lifted a fist in the air. 'Spoken like a true soldier.' He grinned. 'Of course, many a soldier has been brought down by a woman.'

'Aw, shut up!' Brent said. 'Anyway, I thought you were launched on a campaign to win her.'

'You can't win if you don't have a good hand.' Woodcock shrugged. 'Seems I've been dealt a fistful of deuces.'

'Then why are you hanging around so much?'

'Are you blind?' Woodcock snorted. 'As long as I'm hanging around, Voss can't make any headway.'

Brent headed for his blankets. Maybe this was good. A stand-off might keep down trouble.

CHAPTER TEN

Two days later, Brent rode ahead to scout as the herd started up the river. He had moved the herd out some distance toward the bluffs to avoid the rutted trail close to the river.

They were ahead of most of the trains crossing the prairie this summer, but the grass was better away from the ruts cut by last year's caravans.

Brent kept on the look-out for the rider on the gray horse. He knew that Oker Patzel wasn't far away. Brent had only to let down his guard for a moment, and Patzel would strike. The fact that he hadn't seen any sign of Patzel for a few days only increased Brent's alertness.

Brent was back with the herd when it halted for the noon break. A lone rider going east stopped at the wagons and ate with the crew.

'Any Indians to the west?' Brent asked him.

The man shrugged. 'Plenty. But they don't seem to be uncommonly hostile. They'll steal a cow or a horse if they get a chance, but I ain't heard of any big fights.'

'I reckon they'll like the looks of these horses,' Jake Closter said.

The man nodded. 'They sure will. This all the men you've got?'

'Two are out with the herd,' Brent said. 'It will be enough.'

The man shrugged and went on with his dinner.

Brent was just mounting up when he heard Rosene's voice rising sharply at the front of the cook wagon. Looking around quickly, he saw that Woodcock was just riding out of camp, but Voss was nowhere in sight.

Brent swung into the saddle and reined around the wagon. Voss was standing in front of Rosene as though he had just been pushed back, and his face was red with anger.

'Voss, get out to the herd,' Brent snapped.

Voss turned and stared at Brent. 'This is none of your business.'

'You hired on to take this herd to California. That is my business. Now get going.'

Sullenly, Voss turned and shuffled off to his horse. Brent started to ask Rosene what Voss had been up to, then, seeing the angry glint in her eye, decided against it, wheeled his horse and followed Voss.

Toward evening Brent directed the herd into a valley running back into the hills south of the river, where the grass was almost belly deep. Here the horses could be held easily through the night. The wagons came to a halt close to the mouth of the valley.

At supper, Voss moved in beside Rosene as though it were his rightful place. Brent wasn't sure how much encouragement Rosene had given Voss before, but it was obvious that she didn't like his show of possessiveness now. He looked across at Woodcock and got a knowing nod.

Taking his plate, Brent moved over to sit beside Rosene while Voss was filling his plate.

When Voss came back, he scowled at Brent.

'That was my place,' he said angrily. 'Maybe you want to fight me for it?'

Rosene got up angrily. 'You're not going to fight over me. I won't have it!'

'No, we're not going to fight over you,' Brent said softly. 'This is something that was bound to come, anyway.'

'Right after supper,' Voss snapped, and wheeled away to go and sit by Jake and Dickie Closter.

Before Brent finished his meal, Woodcock came by on the way to the wreck pan with his dirty plate.

'You going to scrap with Voss?'

'Looks that way,' Brent said.

'Watch that Dickie,' Woodcock said softly.

Brent nodded. 'Even Jake could stand watching.'

'Where's the fight going to be?'

Brent jerked his head to the west above camp. Woodcock nodded.

'Me and Morrie will be out to see it,' he said, and moved on.

Brent finished his supper and disposed of his dirty dishes. He wondered if Voss would want to fight with guns. Brent was no expert with a gun, but he wasn't the slowest man alive, either. However, he wasn't going to fight Voss with guns. He needed his men too much in the days ahead to risk having someone killed. And a gunshot in the still evening air would carry for miles. Someone might be in earshot whom Brent would rather not alert to the fact that there was trouble in camp.

Brent unbuckled his gun belt and started walking to the west.

Brent saw Voss and Dickie and Jake moving out of the camp together. He was also aware that Woodcock and Morrie were following him. Redmond and Dan Hanson were with the horses now.

Fifty yards beyond the bedrolls, Voss stopped and turned to wait for Brent. When he saw that Brent wasn't wearing a gun, he swore.

'You yellow-bellie coward!' he yelled. 'Where's your gun?'

'At camp where it ought to be,' Brent said evenly. 'I'm not going to kill you. You hired on to help drive those horses, and you're not getting out of it.'

'You knew I'd kill you,' Voss said.

'Hadn't figured on that,' Brent said. 'Now if you want to fight, come on. Let's see if your fists are as big as your mouth.'

Voss hesitated for a moment, his hand only an inch away from his gun. Brent saw that he had underestimated the man. Voss was on the verge of gunning him down even though he was unarmed. With Brent dead, Voss could take over the herd. That was a big prize any way a man looked at it.

Voss shot a glance over at Dickie, and Brent caught the look that passed between them. Brent wished he had kept on his gun. He had walked into a trap without realizing it.

Then, before anybody could make an irreversible decision, Woodcock's voice cut through the stillness.

'I'd keep those hands in sight if I were you,' he said. 'I may not be the best shot in the world, but I'm aiming right at your guts, Dickie. I can't miss you entirely.'

'I'll take anybody else that gets itchy fingers,' Morrie added.

Brent barely stole a glance at the two. They had their guns in their hands, and there was determination in their faces. Woodcock didn't appear unnerved, but Morrie was so nervous he could barely talk. Brent looked back at Voss and Dickie. They realized their danger. A nervous finger on a trigger was far more dangerous than a gun in the hand of a seasoned killer.

'We ain't touching our guns,' Dickie said.

'See that you don't,' Woodcock said. 'Now, Voss, shed that belt and let's see how you make out with the boss.'

Reluctantly, Voss dropped his gun belt. Then he charged toward Brent, all signs of reluctance gone. Brent was ready for him. He had watched him fight Woodcock last night, and he knew his tactics. He had fought brawlers before out in the gold fields of California, and Voss was cut from the same cloth.

Voss was strong, but he wasn't as tall or as heavy as Brent. Brent didn't figure that he was as quick, either. As Voss charged at him, Brent stepped agilely to one side and, with his long reach, slapped a ringing blow on Voss's ear.

Voss turned, glaring at Brent. He knew only one way to fight—charge into the fray, swinging as fast as he could. He charged again, but he kept on the balls of his feet, expecting Brent to dodge to one side. But Brent stood his ground, meeting Voss squarely. He was a little bigger than the cowboy and had a longer reach.

Surprise flashed across Voss's face when he realized that Brent wasn't going to get out of his way. But that surprise gave way quickly to fury and pain as Brent stepped inside Voss's wildly swinging arms and drove his fists into Voss's face. Blood spurted from his nose, and his face twisted grotesquely as Brent's fist caught him on the cheek and jerked his head around.

Voss's fists landed, but they had suddenly lost their power. Brent followed up his advantage, not giving Voss time to recover from the surprise and the punishment he had absorbed in that first exchange.

Brent switched his attack to the cowboy's

chest and stomach, and when Voss's guard involuntarily lowered to protect those areas, he hammered his face again. Voss retreated slowly at first, then faster. His fists were swinging wildly, missing their mark entirely, while Brent was hammering Voss's face into a bloody pulp.

Voss made one last gallant effort to stand his ground, but Brent smashed that effort with a jolting blow to Voss's mouth. Voss backed off again, and Brent sensed the collapse of his confidence. He began retreating rapidly. Brent stopped, because the fight was gone from Voss.

'Let's get things straight, Voss,' Brent said. 'This outfit has only one boss—me. And from now on, leave Rosene alone. If she wants your company, let her ask for it. Is that clear?'

Voss glared at Brent through hate-filled eyes, one of which was rapidly swelling shut. Brent would probably have to deal with that hate later. But at least Voss would be able to work tomorrow.

Voss turned away without a word. Brent knew that if they fought again, it would be with guns.

Brent was plagued with stiff aching muscles when he crawled out of his blankets to take the last shift of night guard. If Voss felt any pain as he was saddling up, he didn't let Brent see it. Brent might have expected him to quit his job if there had been any place for him to go. But out here, his only chance for grub and the safety of numbers was in the crew, and he was smart enough not to throw that away.

Brent passed up the Lower California Crossing in favor of the Upper Crossing. Two guides he had talked to had run into quicksand trouble on the Lower Crossing, and he didn't want any part of that. The Upper Crossing might not be any better, but he hadn't been warned of danger there. He'd have no trouble with the horse herd, but it would be a different matter with the wagons, especially Hanson's old one.

The Upper California Crossing of the South Platte was close to the mouth of Lodgepole Creek. Across the Platte from the Lodgepole on the south bank was a little Indian trading post. A Frenchman, Jules Beni, was the sole operator of the post, and Brent found that the prices he asked were out of reason. Since he still had plenty of supplies, he bought only some strips of rawhide for mending the harness on Dan Hanson's old team.

Brent decided to send the wagons across the river ahead of the herd. He made the crossing first on horseback to look for quicksand bars. A rider could go around the bars, or his horse could struggle out if caught. But a wagon was not so easily maneuvered.

When Brent got back, he put Morrie on his own wagon with instructions to follow him.

Then he plunged into the river again. Morrie followed with his team, and the Hansons came after him. Brent noted with relief that Rosene was handling the reins.

Brent was almost across, with Morrie only twenty yards behind him, when he heard a scream out in the river. Wheeling around in the saddle, he saw that the Hanson wagon was in trouble, apparently stuck in some sand, the horses struggling.

Brent kicked his horse into a trot back through the water. 'Straight ahead, Morrie,' he shouted at his driver as he passed. 'Watch that bar to the left.'

As he neared the Hanson wagon, he saw that only Rosene's calm hands on the reins had prevented a serious accident already. But Dan was standing beside his daughter, trying to jerk the lines out of her hands. If he got the reins and started worrying the team, they'd mire the wagon beyond hope of recovery or else upset the whole outfit.

CHAPTER ELEVEN

'Let her do the driving, Hanson!' Brent shouted as soon as he was close enough to be heard.

'We're stuck,' Hanson yelled back. 'We've got to get out or we'll lose everything we've got.'

Brent splashed up to the wagon. The team had swung to the left a few yards from the course Brent had laid out for the wagons. Flipping his rope free, he tossed one end into the wagon.

'Loop that over the brake lever,' he shouted. 'I'll pull, and you swing the team to the right.'

Rosene, standing in the front of the wagon, pulled the horses' heads to the right, and they floundered, jerking the tongue of the wagon around. Hanson, excited over the struggle, grabbed the closest line from Rosene and jerked on it. The horse reared and lunged downstream, cramping the wheels of the wagon but not jerking them loose from the sand.

'Let go!' Brent shouted, wishing he had made Hanson go with Morrie. The Hanson wagon was overloaded, anyway.

Woodcock came splashing up from the south bank and swung out of the saddle into the water. Throwing his weight against the rear of the wagon, he pushed, while Brent urged his horse forward. Rosene managed to get the team under control again.

On the third effort, the wagon moved a little. Brent shouted over his shoulder as he kept his Morgan straining against the rope. 'Don't let them stop!'

A minute later, the wagon broke free of the

sand and pulled out onto the fairly solid river bottom.

'Follow me,' Brent shouted, and headed toward the north bank, not taking time to flip his rope off the brake lever, although his horse wasn't needed now. The excited Morgans in the harness were more than willing to heave the wagon out of the river.

Once on the bank, Rosene stopped the team, and Brent rode back, flipping his rope off the brake lever and coiling it.

'Guess you didn't lose anything, did you?'

'Pa threw out a couple of boxes of our clothes,' Rosene said.

Brent stared at Dan Hanson. 'What for?'

'We were loaded too heavy,' Hanson said. 'We had to lighten the load.'

'You could have gotten out and pushed,' Brent said disgustedly. 'That would have lightened it considerably.'

Hanson nodded. 'I know it now. I was too excited.'

Brent turned away before his anger exploded.

Leaving the Hansons to take care of the wagons and the teams, Brent took Morrie and Woodcock and rode back to the south side of the river. He had no worries about getting the horse herd across. If they hit a sand bar, they could get out with no trouble.

The horses were grazing peacefully in the rich grass, but they started on the run for the river as soon as the men came at them from the south, shouting and waving ropes in the air.

The herd hit the water at a run, and within twenty minutes all the horses were on the north side, cropping the grass along the banks of the little stream which ran into the South Platte.

Rosene and her mother had dinner almost ready when the riders came in after crossing the herd. Dan Hanson came to meet Brent as he dismounted.

'Can we hold a short prayer meeting of thanksgiving for a safe crossing of the river?'

Brent stared at Hanson. He had almost forgotten that he was a missionary.

'I reckon we're all thankful to get across,' Brent said. 'Go ahead.'

Woodcock and Morrie had stayed with the horses while the others ate, and when Brent explained that dinner would be delayed while Hanson held his prayer meeting, he saw resentment flash in the eyes of the men, especially Jake and Dickie Closter. Hanson had bragged that those two had been converted to his way of thinking. But Brent saw no sign of that now. If Jake and Dickie had been converted, it had been to the religion of the gun rather than Hanson's religion.

'Is this a trail drive or a traveling prayer meeting?' Voss muttered as he passed Brent after Hanson had finished.

Brent said nothing.

As soon as he had finished eating, Brent took Jake and rode out to the herd, sending Morrie and Woodcock in to get their dinner. Shortly after noon, Brent had the herd moving again, leaving the South Platte behind and moving up Lodgepole Creek.

After supper that night, Brent made a swing out to the herd before turning in. He found Woodcock moving along the fringe of the herd, darting his head around like a startled bird.

'Something wrong?' Brent asked.

'Notice the dog,' Woodcock said. 'There's something out there that he doesn't understand.'

Brent looked at the dog close to Woodcock. The other dog apparently was with the other guard. The dog trotted ahead of Woodcock for a while, then stopped, the hair on the back of his neck bristling. Brent thought he detected a low growl as the dog stared out into the growing darkness around the herd.

'What do you figure it is?' Brent asked.

'I don't know,' Woodcock said. 'The dog doesn't know, either. That's what worries me. It could be some animal. Or it could be Indians.'

'Don't tell me you can tell what those dogs are thinking,' Brent said.

'Almost,' Woodcock said. 'I've been with

them for a long time. Dogs are smarter than lots of humans I know. I'll wager all the pay I've got coming that there's something out there.'

'Maybe we should put three men on guard.'

Woodcock shook his head. 'Two should be enough. But whoever is out here with the herd better pay attention to these dogs. If anything tries to sneak up on us, they'll let us know in time to get the rest of the men out here.'

'I'll tell the men to watch the dogs while they're on guard,' Brent said, and reined back to the wagons.

He arranged the guard duty so that he would be on the last shift. If there was to be a dawn attack, he wanted to be the first to know. When he took over his post, the dogs were quiet. He kept one of them with him as he made his rounds.

As the first streaks of dawn lightened the eastern sky, he divided his attention between the dog in front of his horse and the emerging horizon. But the dog trotted along, as unconcerned as if he had never been puzzled by some strange scent or sound last night.

Woodcock and Morrie came out to relieve Brent and Jake so they could get their breakfast.

'Nothing?' Woodcock asked, looking at the dog.

Brent shook his head. 'Whatever it was is gone now.'

'There was something,' Woodcock said. 'If it shows up again tonight, we'd better investigate.'

'And maybe get our hair lifted,' Brent said.

Shortly after sunup, the herd began moving up the little creek again. Brent hoped to camp tonight at the spot where he would turn north toward Courthouse Rock and the North Platte.

It was an hour before noon when the dogs suddenly ran out to the north slope above the creek. Brent cut away from the herd and rode after them. The dogs stopped at the top of the rise, the bristles erect on the backs of their necks. There was no mistaking the growls in their throats when Brent reined up behind them. Woodcock soon came up beside Brent.

'What do you make of that?' Brent asked.

'I don't know. The wind is coming from the north. They hear or smell something that we don't.'

'They don't like whatever it is,' Brent said. He scanned the horizon. 'Can't see a thing.'

'That's the advantage of dogs,' Woodcock said. 'They can smell things a lot farther off than you can see them.'

'Could be Indians, I suppose.'

'Could be,' Woodcock admitted. 'But they act like they hear something. And they tell me you don't hear Indians until it's too late.'

Brent watched the dogs, their heads cocked to one side much as a man might do if he were trying to pick up some sound that was almost too distant or indistinct to be identified.

'Just what could they hear?'

'That's something we'd better find out,' Woodcock said.

Brent hipped around in the saddle and yelled at Al Redmond, who was closest to him. 'Keep the herd moving.'

Then he turned and rode to the north. The dogs quickly took the lead when they saw that the horses were going forward. But they ran carefully and straight to the north. There was no dashing this way and that as they usually did when they picked up an interesting scent in the grass.

Half a mile north of the creek, Woodcock halted his horse. Behind them, the herd was moving almost due west now, following the valley of the Lodgepole.

'We could get too far from the herd, you know,' he said.

Brent reined up, too, and the dogs stopped out in front of them. 'You're right. I'm not too keen about getting cut off from the others.'

'You're thinking it's Indians?'

Brent grinned. 'I'm not afraid of coyotes.'

The dogs stood stiffly, bristles still rising on their necks. They faced north except for an occasional look back to see if the men were going to follow their lead.

'Listen,' Brent said suddenly. 'I think I hear something now, too.'

For a minute both men held their breaths, keeping a tight rein on their horses to prevent them from moving. Brent heard it distinctly now, even though it was so faint it seemed it must be coming from another world. It was a low rumble that he could almost have mistaken for the growl of one of the dogs. But this wasn't a dog.

'What do you make of that?' Woodcock asked, worry in his voice.

Searching the horizon, Brent suddenly pointed. 'Buffalo!' he exclaimed. 'A stampede!'

'And they're heading our way!'

Brent wheeled his horse, and Woodcock followed. They raced back to the creek with the dogs at their heels. From the top of the bluffs above the creek, Brent waved to Redmond to push the horses into a valley that cut into the bluff. It wasn't a high-walled valley, nor were the bluffs steep enough to turn the buffalo stampede, but the big animals might veer around it and follow the ridges. There was no time to look for a safer place.

Racing down to the herd, he quickly passed the word on what had to be done, and Jake Closter, at point, headed into the little side valley. Brent wheeled away from the herd and dashed up the main valley, where the two wagons were keeping in front of the herd, out of the dust.

He reached his own wagon first. Rosene was driving it, with her mother beside her on the seat. Dan Hanson was driving a team of Morgans on his old wagon a couple of hundred yards further up the valley.

'Buffalo stampede coming,' Brent shouted at Rosene. 'Head back to the valley where the horses are.'

Pushing his horse on to Hanson, he repeated the warning. Hanson stared at him for a moment, fear draining the color from his face.

'Get going!' Brent shouted.

Hanson broke into action then and wheeled the team around, slapping the reins furiously.

Brent galloped back toward the horse herd that was being crowded into the little valley. Rosene was only a short distance away now, and Hanson was another three hundred yards behind.

'Get to the head of this gully and try to split the buffalo herd,' Brent shouted at Redmond and Voss.

They spurred their mounts around the horse herd toward the upper end of the gully that led into the valley. Even above the nervous trampling of the horses, Brent could hear the steady roar of the buffalo stampede.

Reining back toward the main valley, he saw that Rosene had her wagon safely at the gully mouth now, but Hanson was still a hundred and fifty yards back.

Suddenly the vanguard of the stampede burst over the bluff. Brent heard Redmond and Voss firing their pistols, and he saw buffalo on both sides of the little valley where the horses were being held, but none in the valley itself.

Hanson's wagon hadn't made it to safety, and Brent realized he wasn't going to make it. His best chance was to turn the wagon straight into the stampede and hope the big animals would go around it. But Hanson stood up in the wagon, whipping his horses into a frenzied run. Crossing in front of the stampede, he had no chance to avoid disaster.

Brent had heard that stampeding buffalo paid no attention to anything ahead of them, but he saw that he'd been misinformed. The charging animals did try to go around the wagon, but the push from behind forced some against the wagon and stopped the horses. One tried to leap over the wagon, but as a jumper, the big brute left something to be desired. He crashed down on the wagon, his heavy front legs splintering the old boards in the wagon bed.

The horses swung around, trying to avoid the crushing weight of the buffalo. Suddenly the tongue of the wagon snapped, and the horses jerked free of the wagon. Turning with the stampede, they moved toward the river, no longer in danger of being trampled to death.

But that left Hanson in a wagon that was rapidly being splintered. Brent spurred his horse out from the safety of the wedge formed by the little valley. Even as he started out, Brent saw the wagon tip and go over on its side from the pressing weight of the buffalo herd.

For a moment Brent reined up. If Hanson would crouch down behind that overturned wagon, he'd probably be safe. But Hanson always panicked when things went wrong. He did it now.

Screaming loudly enough so that the sound carried to Brent over the rumble of the stampede, he headed south with the herd. He wouldn't last fifty yards before being run down. The big animals might try to go around an object as large as a wagon, but they wouldn't turn aside for anything as insignificant as a man.

Spurring his horse at an angle into the herd, Brent rode with the wave of animals, dodging farther into the herd at every opportunity. Dust boiled up from the many hooves, in spite of the heavy grass they were running over. Through the dust, Brent occasionally caught glimpses of Hanson still on his feet, running.

Brent cut over closer to Hanson, fighting his horse's inclination to go with the herd. Just before he reached Hanson, he saw him stumble and fall and a big bull go over the top of him. Brent jabbed his spurs in the Morgan's flanks, and the horse leaped forward, slamming against the hulk of a buffalo cow. The cow moved over, giving ground reluctantly.

The move opened up a small clearing into which Brent shot. He saw Hanson on the ground and kicked his horse over to the north side of him, hoping to force the buffalo to swing around the horse. The front wave of the stampede was past, and the stragglers passing them now were not such aggressive animals. They were only following their leaders, not bulling ahead regardless of any obstacles. They willingly went around Brent's horse rather than bump into him.

Seeing that the horse was going to prove an effective buffer, Brent swung down and knelt beside the missionary. Hanson was breathing, but apparently he had been knocked out when that buffalo bull had hit him. Brent couldn't tell whether or not he had any broken bones.

Standing on the south side of his horse, Brent held his gun in his hand, ready to shoot any buffalo that appeared ready to go over rather than around the horse. But the animals had formed a path around the horse, leaving it and the two men in an island on the prairie.

The late stragglers of the herd were even more reluctant to challenge the horse in their path, and the island got bigger and bigger as the herd thinned out. Then they were gone, and Brent checked Hanson again.

Carefully he lifted him, after convincing himself that no bones were broken, and carried him toward the other wagon at the mouth of the little valley. Rosene and her mother came running to meet him.

'He's out cold,' Brent said, answering their unasked question. 'Can't find any broken bones, but that big bull might have stepped on him. Fix a place in the wagon for him.'

They turned and ran back to the wagon. As soon as Brent had laid Hanson on the makeshift bed, he let Woodcock, who claimed to know a little about doctoring, examine him. Brent went back to the shattered wagon out in the valley. There was very little that could be salvaged. He sent Redmond and Jake to look for the team that Hanson had been driving. He doubted if he'd ever see those two horses or their harness again.

But by mid-afternoon, Redmond and Jake were back with the horses. They had run only a couple of miles and stopped, letting the buffalo go on. Brent had salvaged a few things from the demolished wagon, and Woodcock had declared Hanson the luckiest man alive. There seemed to be nothing wrong with him but a big knot on his head where the buffalo bull apparently had kicked him as he went past.

Most of the things lost were the personal belongings of the Hanson family. The supplies for the drive were in Brent's wagon, which had been saved. Loading the things salvaged from the Hanson wagon into his own wagon, Brent ordered the herd onto the trail again.

'We got through that mighty lucky,' Woodcock said. 'Not a single horse lost. Hanson's wagon wasn't much anyway.'

'When it's all you've got, it's pretty important,' Brent said.

Brent's sympathy for the Hansons was suddenly ripped to shreds as a shot rang out up ahead. They were less than a mile from the spot where the stampede had hit them.

Swinging his eyes to the front of the herd, he saw a dozen horsemen burst over the hill and charge straight at the horse herd.

'Indians!' Voss yelled. 'Take cover!'

CHAPTER TWELVE

The point riders were racing back toward the rear of the herd. Brent spurred his horse to meet them. Already the Indians' shots were swinging the horses toward the river.

'Stop the horses!' Brent shouted. But he saw instantly that he was wasting his breath. The men had panicked in the face of the oncoming Indians. Brent couldn't be sure how many Indians there were, but he estimated there were at least a dozen.

The horse herd, startled by the sudden appearance of the Indians and the shooting over their heads, had wheeled and dashed toward the little creek. Some of the raiders went after them; the rest swung over toward the white men, firing both rifles and hand guns.

Brent found himself alone. He had fired his rifle, and now all he had to shoot was his six-gun. Realizing that he was going to be overrun by the charging Indians, he wheeled his horse and dashed into a small gully running back from the creek. The other men and the wagon were already there. Brent had kept the wagon behind the herd after the buffalo stampede, and now he was glad he had.

Swinging down from his horse, Brent found a spot where he could peek over the top of the ravine and fire at the riders. They had dismounted, too, and taken cover, firing at anyone in the gully who raised his head.

Brent looked at the river, where the horse herd was being chased onto the plateau between the Lodgepole and the South Platte.

It appeared there were perhaps eight or ten men with the herd. The rest had stopped and engaged Brent's crew to keep them from pursuing the horses.

'This is a bloody mess,' Woodcock said, coming up beside Brent. 'I didn't think Indians ever fought like this.'

'Me, neither,' Brent admitted. 'They usually hit and run. But this is well planned. Before we get out of this gully, those horses will be miles from here.'

Redmond left his spot at the gully rim and came over to Brent and Woodcock. 'They ain't fixing to charge us,' he said. 'They just aim to keep us penned up here. Where do you suppose they came from?'

'They could have been after the buffalo herd,' Woodcock said. 'That might have been what stampeded them.'

Brent shook his head. 'Not likely. This raid was planned, and it wasn't part of a buffalo hunt.'

'Shall we make a break to get out of here and go after those horses?' Redmond asked.

Brent looked at the sky. 'It's almost sundown. We'll wait until dark. We'd be picked off like flies if we tried it now. Did everybody get back to this gully all right?'

'Voss and Morrie are over beyond the wagon,' Redmond said. 'The Hansons are all here. I haven't seen Jake or Dickie.'

Brent poked his head up and looked

around. A rifle snapped a shot at him that missed by a wide margin. He fired at the spot where the shot had come from, then ducked back down. 'Keep them busy enough, they won't get ideas about rushing us,' he said.

He hurried over to the wagon. Voss and Morrie had spots close by where they could fire over the top of the bank. Hanson was still lying in the back of the wagon, nursing a headache.

'Have you seen Jake or Dickie?' Brent asked.

Rosene shook her head. 'We turned in here as soon as the shooting started. You five were the only ones who followed us here. Where were Jake and Dickie?'

'Jake was on point; I don't know where Dickie was,' Brent said. 'Maybe they got hit right at the start.'

Woodcock had been riding close to Dickie, but he didn't recall seeing him after the shooting began. Brent decided that Dickie might have tried to defend the herd. Dickie was a fighter, but Brent hadn't expected him to fight to save horses. The only concern he had shown before had been for his own hide.

The sun disappeared. Frequently, Brent raised himself up for a look around and was almost always greeted by the spang of a rifle. The raiders who had been left to keep Brent's crew pinned down were on the job.

Rosene got some food out of the wagon,

and the men took turns going over to get supper. It was a cold meal, for they couldn't risk a fire. That would outline anyone near it and make a perfect target for the raiders out on the rim of the gully.

As soon as it was dark, Brent passed the word that he was going out to survey the possibilities of their breaking out.

'That's a fool thing to do,' Woodcock said. 'You ain't no Indian, and they are. Instead of you sneaking up on them, they'll sneak up on you and lift your hair.'

'Maybe,' Brent said. 'But we can't stay cooped up here much longer if we expect to get those horses back.'

'We ain't going to get them back,' Voss said. 'You might as well make up your mind to that.'

'I'm not giving up,' Brent said. 'I'm going to the head of the gully and try to slip around behind them. If they start shooting, keep them busy.'

'Better take one of the dogs with you,' Woodcock suggested. 'They can sniff them out.'

'I don't need a dog to tell me they're out there,' Brent said. 'Besides, the dog would growl. That would be like blowing a cavalry bugle.'

Brent left the men peering over the top of the gully into the darkness. As he started up the gully, Rosene stopped him.

'Do you think this is wise, Tom?' she whispered.

'Maybe not,' he admitted. 'But it's got to be done. They could keep us bottled up for a week if we just sit here.'

'Won't they leave when they think the horses are far enough away so that you can't catch them?'

'Maybe,' Brent said. 'But I don't figure on staying here that long. I'm going to get those horses back.'

'Be careful, Tom,' she said.

She faded into the darkness, and Brent moved on silently to the head of the gully where it met the level prairie.

For a minute he crouched there, listening. Apparently none of the raiders had heard him leave the camp below. Remembering where the riflemen had been just before dark, Brent moved off to the west to get behind those positions. He had his revolver for emergency use, but he favored a short hunting knife that was in its sheath at his thigh. It was quieter.

Clouds covered the stars. Brent had to depend on his memory to locate the positions of the men he knew were out here. If they had moved, he was in trouble.

He dropped down into the ravine that was to the west of the one where his crew was trapped. Moving along this, he reached a point where he estimated he was behind the rifleman who had the best position overlooking the trapped drovers. He had been the one who usually fired when anyone poked his head up.

Climbing up out of the gully, Brent flattened himself on the prairie suddenly when his foot dislodged a small rock and it skittered to the bottom of the gully. He listened for several seconds. Even though he heard nothing, he felt uneasy. He realized he might not hear an Indian slipping through the darkness to investigate that noise.

Quietly, he rose to his hands and knees and began inching forward. He was sure he was nearing the top of the ridge where the rifleman had been that afternoon. If he was still there, Brent had to surprise him. If any alarm was sounded, he probably wouldn't make it back to the gully.

Brent paused again to listen. The night was deathly still. He heard a horse stamp its foot over in the gully. That would be one of the seven Morgans he had left: the five the crew had been riding and the team Rosene had been driving on the wagon.

Suddenly a soft slithering sound came to him from only a few feet ahead. Brent held his breath. The sound came again, and he identified it as a man's boot sliding along the grass. The sentry must be directly ahead.

Realizing that even the tiniest sound carried far on the night air, Brent began inching forward, lifting each leg and setting it down carefully, doing the same with his hands. Pausing again, he silently unsheathed his knife and held it in his right hand as he moved forward.

He was concentrating so intently on making no sound that a sudden movement within five feet of his face startled him until he almost lunged backward. Steeling himself to immobility, he realized in a moment there was a foot almost in his face. The man was lying full length on the grass, his feet toward Brent. And those feet wore cowboy boots, not moccasins. Brent remembered seeing Indians at Fort Kearny wearing boots. He gripped the knife until his fingers ached as he inched forward.

Suddenly the boots in front of Brent turned over with the toes toward the sky, and the man sat up, facing Brent. Brent reacted instantly, coming out of his crouch, his knife flashing forward to stop against the throat of the man.

'Not a sound,' he hissed.

A startled gulp came from the man, then absolute silence. Brent swallowed his own surprise as he discovered that this was a white man, not an Indian.

'How many more out here?' Brent whispered softly.

'Three,' the man replied after Brent put some pressure on the knife against the man's throat.

'Call them over here,' Brent said. 'Do it easy without making them suspicious. If you don't, you won't live to find out what happens.'

Brent eased the knife back a little from the man's throat, moving around behind him. The man's rifle was on the ground, and Brent found his revolver and dropped it on the grass beside the rifle.

'Ben,' the man said in a low voice, 'call Blackie and Slim and come up here.'

'Got an idea?' someone said out in the darkness.

'Yeah,' the man said after Brent touched his throat again with the knife.

'On your feet,' Brent whispered, then stood behind the man after he got up, keeping the knife against his throat. 'Remember, no mistakes. I'll keep this knife at your throat, and I've got a gun in my other hand.'

It seemed like an eternity before three figures materialized out of the darkness.

'What's on your mind, Judd?' one asked.

Then the man discovered the situation, and Brent spoke quickly. 'Don't get any wild ideas. Come up closer where I can see you better. If anybody does anything foolish, this fellow gets his throat cut. I've got a gun on the rest of you.'

Brent knew the ones in the back could duck into the darkness, and he'd never be able to hit them. But he was depending on the threat to the man he held to keep them momentarily undecided.

The lead man stepped forward hesitantly. Brent spoke in the ear of the man he was holding. 'Tell them to come up one at a time and drop their guns at your feet. If you want to live, they'd better do it.'

The man's voice was shaky, but he obeyed, and the three men, apparently not sure whether they should fight or follow orders, moved up reluctantly and shed their guns. Only then did Brent take the knife from the man's throat.

'Now then, stand close together,' he ordered, waving his gun so that they could see it even in the dim light.

When they were close together, he ordered them to move slowly toward the gully. There might be more men behind him, but he had to take that chance. As he got close to the gully, he called to Woodcock.

'I'm coming in, Woodie. Don't shoot.'

They were almost at the brink of the gully before he saw the men waiting for them. The captives climbed down into the gully under a ring of guns.

'Tie them up, Morrie,' Brent said. 'Do a good job; then we'll post a guard over them.'

'How did you do it?' Woodcock asked in amazement. 'Is this all of them?'

'According to that one, this is all,' Brent said, indicating the man he had first captured.

'I'm going back and get their guns.'

When Brent returned with the rifles and revolvers, he found that Redmond and Morrie had tied the four men with the ropes from their saddles, one man to each wheel of the wagon.

'Can we have a fire?' Voss asked.

'Better not,' Brent said. 'Could be that jasper was lying. One man could pick us off pretty fast if we have a fire behind us.'

'Do you realize there's not one Indian among those four?' Woodcock asked Brent.

Brent nodded, but Redmond spoke up. 'There were Indians in that gang that hit us. I know an Indian when I see one.'

'It looked like Indians driving the horse herd away,' Brent admitted. 'But they sure had white help.'

'Now that we've got these horse thieves out of the way, let's go after our horses,' Morrie said impatiently.

'We can't track them tonight. You can hardly see your hand before your face.'

'We saw which way they went.'

'We saw which way they started. They may not keep going that way. We'll start at dawn.'

CHAPTER THIRTEEN

All the next day, Brent rode with Woodcock, Voss, Redmond and Dickie Closter. When the sun sank out of sight, Brent called a halt only long enough for the men to eat some cold meat and bread from their saddle bags; then he led the way up the river.

The sky was clear, and there was just a sliver of a new moon above the western horizon. But it gave very little light. The stars outshone it.

'Watch your horses,' Brent advised the others. 'If we get close enough to the herd so that these horses can smell them, they'll try to whinny.'

It was Brent's Morgan that caught the first scent of the horses up ahead. He jerked up his head and drew in his breath. Brent lunged over the saddle horn and clamped a hand over his horse's nose.

'They must be close,' he said softly. 'We'll hold up here. Don't let the horses make a sound. I'm going ahead on foot.'

'They could have a guard out,' Dickie warned.

'I figure they will,' Brent said. 'I don't intend to get close; just near enough so that I can locate the horses. We'll hit them at dawn.'

'Nothing like playing Indian with Indians,' Redmond said, dismounting and reaching up for Brent's reins.

Brent swung down and hurried forward, trying to walk quietly. But that was difficult when it was so dark. The moon was gone now, and only the light of the stars struggled to pierce the shadows.

Brent had gone only a hundred yards, however, when he stopped suddenly, arrested by sounds up ahead. For a minute he held his breath until he had identified the sound as the soft rip of tearing grass as animals grazed. Then came the sound of a trot as one of the animals got nudged away from his place and moved to another open area. That trot told Brent that there were horses, not cattle or buffalo ahead. The breeze was coming from the west, bringing the sound toward him and keeping his own scent away from the horses.

Brent went no closer. There were several horses just ahead. That was either the herd he was looking for or else a big Indian village. If it was a village, the Morgans were probably there, too.

Moving quietly back to the rest of his men, he explained in a whisper what he had found.

'How many Indians?' Woodcock asked.

'Didn't see any or I wouldn't be here now,' Brent said. 'But they're there, all right. Woodie, you keep Al and Kyle here with you. I'll take Dickie, and we'll circle around and come in from above them just at dawn. If we hit them by surprise, maybe we can get the horses away before they have time to scatter them. Head them north. If those horses get across the river, we may never get them back.'

'What if those thieves have a lot of other Indians with them by now?' Redmond asked.

'We still want those horses,' Brent said. 'Wait till Dickie and I open up on them. With this breeze from the west, we'll have to stay back farther or the horses will smell us. Any questions?'

'When are you leaving?' Woodcock asked.

Brent took out his pocket watch and held it close to his eyes. 'It's after one now,' he said. 'Dickie and I will move out in about an hour. We'll have to take a long way around so they won't hear us.'

Brent got another chunk of cold meat from his saddle bag and ate it while he waited, noting that the others did the same. Dickie didn't have anything, and Brent shared a chunk of meat and bread with him.

When he guessed that there were still about two hours before dawn, Brent led Dickie off straight north. A mile or more out, he swung to the west and rode another couple of miles before turning south again. They reached the river before any streaks of dawn appeared. There, Brent called a halt and dismounted.

'Can't risk getting any closer,' he said. 'The

breeze is behind us.'

'I don't figure this is an Indian village,' Dickie said. 'There'd be dogs barking if it was.'

Brent recognized the truth of that. 'How many Indians are with the horses?

'If they haven't picked up any more, there won't be more than eight or ten,' Dickie said. 'At least, that's all Jake and me saw before we were jumped.'

Ten minutes later, Brent pointed to the eastern sky. 'Starting to get light. Let's go.'

Dickie nodded. 'Just make sure it's light enough to see all the varmints before we let them know we're here.'

Brent led the way on foot, leading his horse, one hand on the bridle where he could stop a whinny if the horse decided to greet his brethren ahead. By the time they were close enough to see the herd, the light was much stronger, and Brent could make out the Indians' camp down close to the river. The horses were spread out over the rich bottomland grass and up on the slopes to the north.

No alarm had sounded in the camp yet, and Brent moved to the north, where a little ridge running out from the hills cut them off from view of the camp. Peering over the top of this ridge, Brent watched the camp come alive as the Indians started stirring around. Looking downstream, he finally caught sight of Woodcock moving up.

'Let's go,' he said to Dickie.

Mounting, Brent lifted his revolver and kicked his horse into a run. His rifle wouldn't be much use to him here. It had only one shot, and he hoped to get within six-gun range before he started shooting.

Dickie was right at his heels as he thundered around the end of the ridge and straight at the Indian camp. A shout went up from the camp, and Brent wasted one shot to let Woodcock know that the ball had opened.

The Indians grabbed rifles and fired wildly, but in the uncertain light, they didn't come close to their targets. Then, as Brent and Dickie got close enough to make their shots count, they opened up. Only two of the Indians had revolvers. They were firing recklessly, while the others, who had emptied their rifles, were running for their horses.

Brent rode toward the Indians, who were trying to get mounted, while Dickie bored straight in on the two firing the revolvers. In a moment the two revolvers were silent, while the other Indians, five if Brent could count well enough in the confusion, managed to get on their horses.

They headed straight for the river, apparently willing to let the horse herd go in order to save their hides. Brent looked around at Dickie. He was on the ground, examining the two Indians he had shot. Up ahead,

Woodcock and Redmond and Voss were boring in on the camp from the east. Voss suddenly veered off to the north, where the Indian who had been guarding the herd was trying to escape. He had a good lead on Voss, but Voss suddenly jerked his horse to a stop and leaped out of the saddle, yanking his rifle from its boot. Taking careful aim over the saddle, he fired, and the Indian threw up his hands and slid off his horse.

Brent looked around for other Indian guards but didn't see any. The Morgans were dashing around in excitement, bumping into each other in their effort to find a way out to a place where there was no shooting. After Voss's last shot, it was quiet to the north, and the horses lined out that way, running hard.

'Are we going to get them?' Dickie shouted, indicating the five Indians splashing across the river.

Brent looked at the Indians, then at the horses streaming to the north. 'We'd better get the horses. Let the Indians go.'

'They could bring the whole tribe after us,' Dickie warned.

'If we chase them, we could lose all the horses,' Brent said. 'Let's go.'

He spurred his horse after the herd disappearing into the hills and valleys to the north, motioning for Woodcock and his men to follow. They thundered out of the valley after the horses, letting the Indians who had escaped disappear to the south across the river.

It was five miles before they began to catch up with the herd. There the stragglers had stopped to eat, and the riders pushed them along to catch up with the rest. Brent spread his men out in a wide semicircle to pick up any horses that might have wandered away from the main herd. But they found very few. Most of the horses had stayed together.

'Look for any trouble from those Indians that got away?' Woodcock asked as they pointed the herd northeast towards Lodgepole Creek, where they had left the wagon.

'I hope not,' Brent said. 'At least it will be a while before they can round up enough braves to come after us.'

'They may not give up the idea of owning these horses,' Woodcock said worriedly. 'I hope nothing happened back at camp. I didn't like leaving Morrie in charge of those four killers.'

Brent nodded, saying nothing. He hadn't liked that, either.

He kicked his horse into a run, then suddenly reined down to a trot as he realized he was letting his imagination run away with him. Nothing had happened, he told himself. Morrie would keep a close guard on the prisoners, and Patzel wasn't likely to come looking for them. He'd figure they were just doing their job of keeping Brent and his men pinned down while Jake and Dickie helped the Indians run the horses off. If Patzel checked on anybody, it would be on Jake and Dickie to see why they hadn't brought the Morgans to him.

But the nagging worry persisted. He'd left two women, an excitable old man and a boy to watch four men who had to be pretty tough customers if they rode with Patzel.

He pushed the horse herd along, not giving the horses any time to eat as they went. Woodcock rode over in mid-afternoon and reined in beside him.

'You must figure those Indians are right on our tail,' he said.

Brent shook his head. 'I'm worried about the camp back on the Lodgepole.'

Woodcock studied his face for a moment, then grinned. 'Why don't you say what's really worrying you? You're afraid something will happen to Rosene?'

'I'm afraid something will happen to all of them,' Brent snapped.

Woodcock's grin widened. 'Sure, I know. You'd cry your eyes out if Dan Hanson ran a sliver under his fingernail, but you wouldn't bat an eye if those men escaped and ran off with Rosene.'

'Aw, shut up,' Brent said.

Woodcock glanced at the sun. 'Figure we can make it back tonight?'

Brent nodded. 'I reckon. The Indians only had a couple of hours of daylight that first day, then all day yesterday to get as far as they've gone. We're cutting across. We should make it in one day.'

'If we don't wear the legs off these horses,' Woodcock muttered.

The herd hit Lodgepole Creek shortly before sundown, and a quick glance told Brent that he hadn't seen this section of the creek on this trip. So they were above the gully where he had left the camp.

Turning the horses downstream, he pushed them harder than ever. Shortly after sundown, Brent, riding point now, saw the gully. The wagon was still there, but he didn't see any sign of life. Spurring his horse into a run, he headed for the gully.

Suddenly Morrie ran out from the gully. Brent pulled his horse to a halt beside Morrie, his eyes searching the gully behind him.

'Is everything all right?' he asked.

'We don't have any prisoners or horses,' Morrie said.

'What happened?'

'The prisoners escaped. I guess one of them got loose somehow, and he let the others loose. I see you got the horses.'

Brent nodded. 'Where did they go?'

'I don't know,' Morrie said. 'They took every horse we had, including their own, which I went out and brought in yesterday morning. We're afoot.'

'We've got plenty of horses,' Brent said in relief. 'I was afraid they might kill you if they got loose.'

'They didn't have any guns,' Morrie said. 'They just sneaked out and caught four horses, then stampeded the rest. I took some shots at them, but I don't think I hit anybody.'

'Wasn't anybody guarding them?'

'It was Dan's turn. I figure he went to sleep. He says they just slipped away and he didn't see them. It was pretty dark last night, you know.'

Brent sighed. 'Well, it can't be helped now. You're safe, and we did get the horses back. We'll catch another team to pull the wagon and a horse for you to ride. Can you get any grub for us? We're starved.'

Brent placed a heavy guard on the horses through the night. He could expect trouble from Patzel any time now. He had struck once; he wouldn't wait long to try again. In a few days Brent would have the herd at Fort Laramie, where his brother Bill was to meet him with more men to help get the herd over the mountains and down into California. Patzel would strike before Brent got to Fort Laramie.

Moving out shortly after sunup the next morning, Brent turned the herd north before noon and headed toward Courthouse Rock.

They'd have to make a dry camp tonight, but he had made sure the herd was well watered before leaving the Lodgepole.

After camp was made that night, Dickie came over to Brent. 'Going to camp by Courthouse Rock tomorrow night?'

Brent looked sharply at Dickie. Everything Dickie said sounded suspicious to Brent now. He shook his head. 'There's no water at the rock. We'll go north to the river.'

Dickie and Voss got into an argument just before the crew turned in, and Brent thought he was going to have to separate them. He tried to find out what their argument was about, but both men shut up like stone statues.

The herd was moving again by sunup the next morning. There was no water for the horses, and Brent intended to get to water before thirst made them too hard to handle.

Before noon, the horses became unruly, breaking into runs now and then, snorting the dust out of their nostrils and whinnying for water. Rosene took the horse Brent had saddled and tied it behind the wagon for emergency use and rode out to the herd.

'Pa can handle the wagon,' she told Brent. 'I think you're going to need every rider you can get.'

'Without Jake, we are short-handed,' Brent agreed. 'Soon as we get to the river, we'll be all right.'

Rosene pointed to a big rock jutting out of the horizon ahead and a little to the left. A smaller rock was close to it. 'Is that Courthouse Rock?'

Brent nodded. 'That's it. Jail Rock is right by it. But the river is a few miles farther on.'

'Do you think those Indians will hit again?'

'It's not the Indians that worry me. It's the men that we captured who got away.'

'You'll get us through,' Rosene said.

CHAPTER FOURTEEN

As the herd approached Courthouse Rock, Brent left the horses, which were moving steadily now, and rode ahead to scout the area. Although he found nothing at the rock, he stayed there as the herd trotted by on its way to the river to the north.

The horses broke into a run when they smelled the water. Brent let them go. It was late in the afternoon when the horses had quenched their thirst. Brent set up camp a short distance from the river.

With supper over, he rode around the herd with the first night guard, then came back to the camp. He found Voss saddling his horse.

'Just where are you going?' he demanded. 'You don't go on guard till two o'clock.'

'I'm going after a weasel that slipped out of

camp.'

Brent looked over the horses that had been caught up for night use. Dickie's was gone. 'Where did he go?'

'That's what I intend to find out,' Voss said.

'I'm short of men right now.'

Voss swung into the saddle. 'You might be shorter if I find Dickie.'

Before Brent could stop him, Voss was gone into the night, spurring his horse into a gallop. Brent stared into the darkness where Voss had disappeared. He didn't trust Dickie an inch. And he didn't trust Voss much farther. He'd be safer without either one in the crew, he was sure. But he simply didn't have enough men to handle the herd without them.

Worriedly he headed for his bedroll. Where could Dickie have gone? The answer was so obvious that Brent couldn't ignore it. There was only one man who would have any reason for following the herd—Oker Patzel. Dickie must have gone to see him.

Brent didn't sleep before it was his turn to ride guard. Neither Voss nor Dickie were back, and Dickie was scheduled to ride on this shift. Brent called Woodcock, who was slated to take the last guard before morning. They rode out and relieved Morrie and Redmond.

'Going to make a long night of riding for

me,' Woodcock said, yawning. 'Voss and I have the last shift.'

'I'll take that shift with Voss if he gets back,' Brent said. 'I need two men out here all the time.'

'That's no fooling,' Woodcock said. 'I heard Dickie leave about dark. I don't trust that fellow any further than I would a rattler.'

When it was time for the third shift to take over, Brent left Woodcock at the herd while he rode into camp. He was surprised to find both Dickie and Voss in their blankets. He had felt that one or the other of the men would never come back to the camp. He shook Voss awake.

'Time to hit the leather,' he said. 'Your shift.'

Without a word, Voss pulled on his boots and headed for his horse. Brent followed him.

'Where did Dickie go?' he asked when they were out of earshot of the camp.

'Don't know,' Voss said sullenly. 'He gave me the slip. He's like a rattler in the rocks. I finally gave up and came back. He was rolled up in his blankets like he'd been there all night.'

'You didn't see anybody out there that he might have met?'

Voss shook his head. 'I rode back to Courthouse Rock and all around it, but I didn't see anything.'

'He didn't ride off just for the exercise.'

'You and me both know that.'

Voss swung into the saddle and kicked his horse into a trot toward the herd. Brent followed him, sending Woodcock back to camp for some more sleep. Even though he didn't trust Voss, he was sure that he would keep his eyes open tonight. For some reason that Brent wasn't sure of, Voss hated Dickie like poison, and he wouldn't let Dickie get away with stealing the herd if he could help it.

Brent got the herd on the trail early the next morning, even though he was so tired he could hardly sit in the saddle. He might have to take a chance on Dan Hanson on guard duty tonight. Hanson had volunteered to take his turn. Brent didn't trust him to keep alert, but he might do all right if he had a good man with him.

When they stopped at noon, they were within a short distance of Chimney Rock. After Rosene had filled all the other plates, she brought her own and sat down beside Brent.

'Wish we could ride over to that rock as we pass,' she said.

'Maybe we can,' Brent said. 'We'll be pretty close to it. A lot of people have scratched their names on the base of that as they passed here the last three or four years.'

'I'd like to add mine,' Rosene said. 'Will you go with me?'

Brent nodded. 'I sure won't let you go alone. We'll put our names together.'

Their meal was interrupted suddenly by a commotion at the far side of the camp. Brent shot a glance that way then set his plate down.

Dickie and Voss were on their feet, apparently involved in another argument. They usually managed to get off by themselves for their disagreements, so nobody really knew what they were arguing about. But one glance told Brent that this argument was rapidly getting out of hand.

Getting to his feet, he hurried that way. Redmond was on his feet, too, and he caught Brent's arm as he went past.

'It's been coming for a long time. If you say so, I'll pitch in and help Kyle.'

'You think Voss is right?' Brent asked.

'I ain't sure anybody's right,' Redmond said, and Brent had the feeling he was leaving a lot unsaid. 'But they sure are going to kill one another if we let them go.'

'You just stopped me from interfering.'

Redmond nodded. 'You can't do anything unless you're willing to take sides with guns.'

Brent switched his eyes back to the two men. They were thirty feet apart now, and each was throwing curses at the other.

It was Voss who finally broke and clawed for his gun. But it was Dickie who got his gun out of the holster first. His draw was as swift as an eagle's strike, and his aim was deadly. Voss barely got his shot off before he sprawled full length in the grass. Redmond's hand dropped to his gun, but Brent caught it. Dickie had already switched his eyes to Redmond. Everybody knew that Voss and Redmond had been together much of the time, and if Dickie had any trouble with any of the rest of the crew, it would be Redmond.

'Now don't any of you get itchy fingers,' Dickie said sharply as he stared around at the other men. 'I wouldn't mind leaving some more of you dead.'

Keeping his gun in his hand, he circled to the horses and got his. 'Morrie,' he called, 'get my bedroll out of the wagon and bring it here.'

'You leaving?' Brent asked.

'I am unless somebody wants to try to stop me.'

'Where will you go? What about your pay?'

'I'll make out,' Dickie said.

'I'll bet he will,' Redmond said softly.

Morrie got the bedroll, took it over close to Dickie and dropped it. Dickie tied it on behind his saddle while the others watched; then he mounted and rode to the southwest toward Chimney Rock.

'Where will he go?' Woodcock asked.

'To join up with the horse thieves,' Redmond said. 'Let's see about Kyle.'

He ran to Voss, but after a moment, he

turned to face Brent. 'He's dead. We'll have to bury him.'

It took an hour, and Brent forgot all about riding to Chimney Rock with Rosene to carve their names on the rock. Rosene didn't mention it, either. The tragedy in camp had dampened her enthusiasm, too.

Brent took a look at his crew as he started the herd west again. Only five men now, counting Dan Hanson, and two women. Even with the two dogs, they could hardly handle the herd if any crisis came up.

They didn't move too far beyond Chimney Rock before Brent called a halt for camp. He had selected a pocket in the bluffs to the south where the herd would be held during the night. It would be much easier to keep a close watch over the horses there than it would be out on the flat prairie.

Before Brent left the natural corral, Al Redmond reined his horse over to him.

'We're in a real tight spot now,' he said. 'Short-handed, and we're sure to run into trouble ahead.'

Brent nodded. 'I know. Did Voss ever say anything about his trouble with Dickie?'

Redmond nodded. 'I figure you've got a right to know about that, too. I hooked on with Voss back in Westport Landing. We took quite a shine to each other. I'd come from St. Louis and Voss had been to California and come back dead broke. Just before we got together, he'd been contacted by some man who offered him a good price if he'd hook on with you and this horse herd and help him grab the herd somewhere out here on the plains.'

'Oker Patzel?' Brent asked.

Redmond nodded. He swung off his horse and began rolling a smoke. Brent dismounted, too, keeping one eye on the horses grazing in the gully.

'It wasn't just by chance that you stumbled onto us back there in Westport. I told Kyle I didn't want any part of a double-cross, but I did want to get to California, so I went along with his scheme. I was to go with the herd to California. Then Dickie and Jake showed up. I don't know who Jake was, but Dickie is Sam Dicky, the gunman, Kyle said.'

'Then Voss must have known he wouldn't stand a chance trying to gun him down.'

'Yeah, I reckon he did. But he was so mad at Dickie that he didn't care. You see, this Patzel found Dickie and Jake and decided they were a better bet to get the herd from you than Kyle and me, so he switched to them. That left Kyle out in the cold, and he didn't take kindly to that.'

'Was that raid back on the Lodgepole Dickie's idea?' Brent asked.

'Yeah. That didn't set well with Kyle, either. He didn't know a thing about it until it happened. The plan was for the Indians to steal the horses while four of Patzel's men held us there in the gully. Dickie and Jake were to go after the Indians and take the horses back to Patzel. But the Indians liked those horses, too, and they decided they'd keep them. That's when the shooting started and Jake got killed. Dickie didn't lie too much about that.'

'Where has Dickie gone now?'

'To meet Patzel, I'd guess. Kyle told me that Dickie said they were going to grab the herd before you got to Fort Laramie. Seems Patzel has heard that your brother is to meet you there with more men. It will be easier to get the horses before that.'

Brent nodded. 'It sure will. Now that we're three men short, it will be mighty easy.'

'Are you going to tell the others?'

Brent nodded. 'They deserve a chance to save their lives. It's suicide to stick with me now. They can head back to hook up with a wagon train. That's the only sensible thing for them to do. You, too.'

Redmond shook his head. 'Not me. Kyle was a friend of mine, even if he was a two-faced renegade. I've got a score to settle with Sam Dicky. The best chance I'll have of seeing Dickie again is to stick with this herd.'

Brent swung back into the saddle. He assigned Morrie to keep an eye on the herd.

Everyone else was in camp when Brent and Redmond rode in. Rosene and her mother had supper almost ready. Brent called them all close to the fire.

'You know who has been trying to get these horses, and I think you know why,' he said. 'Al has just told me that he found out that Dickie works for Oker Patzel and has very likely gone now to report to him that we're three men short of what we had just a few days ago. Al also said that Patzel plans to hit this herd before we get to Fort Laramie. That could be any time now.'

'What are we going to do?' Hanson asked.

'I'm telling you what to expect so you can decide what to do,' Brent said.

'How many men has this Patzel got?' Woodcock asked.

Brent looked at Redmond, and the tall cowboy shrugged.

'Kyle never said, and I don't reckon he knew,' Redmond said. 'He has plenty, you can be sure of that. Besides Patzel himself, we know he has four gunnies, because we had that many tied up in that gully down on the Lodgepole. Now Dickie is with them. So that makes six, at the very least.'

'And there's only five of us, counting everybody,' Woodcock said.

'You're not counting everybody,' Rosene said sharply. 'Ma and I count for something.'

'I mean in a fight,' Woodcock said uncomfortably.

'Besides, we'll have the horses to take care

of,' Hanson added gloomily.

'I think the best thing for you, Dan, is to take your women and go back till you meet a wagon train. You can hook up with them. Patzel doesn't want you—just these horses.'

'Are you going back?' Rosene asked.

Brent shook his head. 'These horses wouldn't do me any good back in Westport.'

Brent looked at Dan Hanson and noticed that the others were doing the same. Hanson shifted his feet uncomfortably.

'We'll stay with you. You need us now.'

Brent wasn't sure he liked that decision.

'Think it over till morning,' he suggested, seeing the uncertainty still on Hanson's face.

Brent divided the night between two guards, himself and Redmond on one shift, Morrie and Woodcock on the other. Rosene offered to take a turn, but Brent refused. And he didn't figure Dan Hanson would be any better out there than an empty saddle.

Wearily, they moved out the next morning.

Rosene drove the wagon this morning, with her mother riding beside her. Dan Hanson rode with the men, and Brent had to admit he could hold his own driving the herd as long as nothing went wrong.

When they stopped for dinner, Woodcock came over with his plate to sit beside Brent. 'Know what Hanson wants to do now?'

'No telling,' Brent said, taking a bite of beans.

'He wants to ride out to meet Patzel as soon as we can find him and try to convince him that violence never settled anything.'

'We'll have to keep a tight rein on him,' Brent said.

Shortly after noon, Brent, riding ahead of the herd, came to the place where the wagon trail swung to the south to get around the bluffs and canyons close to Scott's Bluff. The trail went south over what was called Robideau Pass, although Brent remembered that it wasn't much of a pass out there, just a gentle slope. He was sure he could take the herd straight ahead and get through the bluffs, but he might have trouble getting the wagon through. So he guided the herd to the southwest around the bluffs.

Leaving Woodcock in charge of the herd, Brent rode a couple of miles ahead to scout for trouble. This was the kind of country he would pick to hit the herd if he were in Patzel's place. If Brent had kept the herd on the river, there would have been lots of places for an ambush. Out here there were fewer places, but it was still rough country.

Brent was far in advance of the herd when he caught the glint of the afternoon sun on metal and reined up sharply. A moment later, he saw two riders come over a ridge a half-mile ahead of him. Within a few seconds a half-dozen more riders came over the ridge. Brent needed only one look to know they weren't Indians. He could see the big hats, and a couple of the men had rifles across their saddles.

They reined up sharply when they saw Brent, apparently more surprised than he was. Then suddenly they swept forward like an ocean wave. Brent wheeled his horse and dug in the spurs. Patzel's men had chosen this place to strike at the herd, but Brent had taken away their surprise.

As soon as he came within sight of Woodcock, riding point, he stood in his stirrups and waved his hat toward the bluffs along the river. Woodcock waved back in reply.

It would be a furious chase to the river, and Brent doubted he could win.

CHAPTER FIFTEEN

Brent angled to the northeast to catch up with the horse herd. He had instructed Rosene to keep the wagon behind the herd today, figuring there was less danger there than up in front. Now he saw Rosene whipping her team into a run, almost keeping up with the herd as it dashed north.

Brent came to the breaks along the river and found himself cut off from the valley floor by steep walls hemming in a small canyon. He had to circle back to the south to get around it. Woodcock had been more fortunate in his choice of direction, for the horses hit the breaks at the head of a gentle draw that led them right down to the river.

Brent caught up with Woodcock as they hit the flat river bottom. Just to the west loomed Scott's Bluff, with many smaller bluffs ranging back from the river. The wagon was coming down the gully the herd had just descended.

'Head them west,' Brent shouted. 'I saw a canyon up there where we can hold them.'

He spurred his horse to the west to find the mouth of the steep-walled gully, and when he found it, he reined around to guide the horses into it. Morrie thundered past the running horses to take up a stand close to Brent and help turn the herd.

The horses were not hard to swerve into the canyon, and it didn't appear to Brent that they had lost any on the run. He yelled for the men to hold them while he spurred his horse back toward the wagon. He had gone only a couple of hundred yards when he saw the wagon careering toward him, Rosene standing in the front shaking the reins.

Brent reined up until the wagon was close, then motioned for Rosene to follow him. He didn't know how far away Patzel and his men were, but it couldn't be far.

When the wagon turned into the gully,

Brent heard the men shouting at the horses. Apparently the animals had discovered they were in a box canyon and had turned back to get out. Two hundred yards inside the little canyon, Brent came on the men trying to calm the horses and keep them from breaking out into the valley again. The horses had had a hard run and soon gave up trying to break out. Woodcock had put the dogs to work, and they soon discouraged even the most persistent horses from trying to escape from the canyon.

'If they come straight toward us, they'll show up on the rim,' Brent shouted to the men. 'Morrie, you watch the west wall. Woodie, watch the east. Al and I and Dan will keep them out of the mouth of the gully.'

Brent directed the wagon to a spot close to the east rim of the gully and helped unhitch the horses. Before he had finished, he heard Morrie open up with his rifle. Looking up, he saw riders on the rim to the west. They didn't fire back at Morrie, but they sent some shots down toward the wagon.

'Get up closer to the herd,' Brent shouted to Dan. 'Rosene, you and your mother get under the wagon.'

'We might get trampled by those horses if we get too close,' Hanson objected, panic in his voice.

'They won't hurt those horses,' Brent said. 'They intend to steal them, and they don't want cripples.'

Within minutes, Brent was sure that he had guessed right. Patzel wouldn't shoot at any target close to one of the Morgans. He evidently was supremely confident that he could get the horses without risking injury to them.

Brush choked the mouth of the canyon, but it had been severely trampled close to the horse herd. Still, it offered fairly good protection for the men below, while the men above had to expose themselves to get a shot down into the gully. Brent was sure he hit one man when he leaned over the rim to shoot down. The shooting from above stopped shortly after that.

'What do you make of this quiet?' Woodcock asked, coming over close to Brent.

'They're going to figure out some safer way of getting to us,' Brent said. 'They can't shoot accurately straight down, anyway.'

'I sure didn't figure we'd have a chance when they struck at us,' Woodcock said.

'We're lucky. But we're still pinned down here until they decide how to get to us.'

'They can't ride down those walls,' Woodcock said. 'And I don't figure they'll try sneaking down on foot.'

'They might after dark,' Brent said. 'But we'll be watching for them.'

Woodcock nodded. 'We'll patrol the walls with the dogs. They'll tell us if anybody's trying to sneak in.'

Suddenly a loud voice boomed over the canyon, coming from the rim.

'Hey, Brent, you're trapped down there. We'll let you go if you'll ride out and leave the horses.'

'That's Patzel,' Brent said to Woodcock.

'We'd better take him up on that,' Hanson said. 'It's the only way we'll get out of here alive.'

'You don't think he'd let us go to bring charges against him in California, do you?' Brent asked.

'You mean you think he'd kill us after we left him the horses?' Hanson asked in disbelief.

Brent nodded. 'I'm sure of it. He'd let us ride out of the canyon to where he could shoot at us without hurting the horses. But that's as far as we'd get. Of course, he might let you and your family go, since you have never seen Patzel and couldn't identify them.'

'What about it, Brent?' Patzel shouted from the rim.

Brent searched the rim but couldn't see anything. Patzel was staying safely back out of sight

'There's only one way you'll get these horses, Patzel,' Brent shouted. 'That's to come down here and take them.'

'That's up to you,' Patzel shouted. 'One thing sure, you're not going to come out of there with them.'

There wasn't a sound in the canyon for the next ten minutes except for the restless tramping of the horses.

'This is getting on my nerves,' Morrie said. 'I wish they'd do something.'

'They will soon enough,' Brent said. 'They're probably figuring out just what to do. I don't think they'll try much more shooting over the rim. They're at a disadvantage there.'

'I'm going up to the head of the canyon to make sure they don't try sneaking down there,' Woodcock said.

'Good idea,' Brent said. 'Morrie, you keep an eye on the west rim. Al, you watch the other rim.'

'How about some supper?' Rosene asked. 'They won't shoot us while we cook, will they?'

'I doubt it,' Brent said. 'But stay back close to the bluff.'

Dan Hanson helped his wife and daughter get ready to make supper.

Brent was concentrating on the west wall, where Patzel's men had last been seen, when suddenly he heard a sharp scuffle behind him at the wagon. Wheeling, he saw some man wrestling with Rosene. She was at the back of the wagon, apparently getting some food for supper. Dan Hanson had built the fire several yards away under an overhang in the bluff, and he and his wife were there. The sun was down already, and it was getting gloomy in the canyon, but Brent could easily distinguish what was happening.

Dashing toward the wagon, Brent reached it just as the man got Rosene's arms pinned to her sides. In that instant, Brent recognized Dickie.

So far, Rosene had kept Dickie too busy for him to look around. But now he saw Brent, and one hand let go of Rosene's arm as it dived for his gun. Rosene brought her arm forward, than back with all the force she had, jamming her elbow into Dickie's stomach.

Breath exploded from Dickie, and he involuntarily backed off a step. His hand stopped its downward arc. In that instant Brent reached him. Grabbing a shoulder, he jerked the gunman from Rosene, but Rosene was thrown to the ground before Dickie's grip was torn loose.

As Brent's fist connected solidly with the side of Dickie's face, he felt satisfaction race through him. Dickie staggered back but didn't go down. Brent followed him closely. He knew he didn't dare give him a chance to pull his gun.

Dickie tried to reach his gun even as he was staggering back, and Brent hit him once more. He followed, hitting him again, as they moved away from the wagon. He was dimly aware of running feet behind him, but he didn't dare glance around to see if it was reinforcements for him or for Dickie.

Dickie continued to retreat, barely fighting back as he concentrated on getting his gun in his hand. Brent was just as dedicated to keeping him from doing it.

Then Dickie got his feet tangled in some brush and went down on his back. Even that didn't interrupt his determination to get his gun. His fingers clawed for his gun and pulled it free of the leather.

Before he could squeeze the trigger, however, a shot rang out, and Dickie was thrown into a convulsion on the ground. Three more shots followed the first. With each one, Dickie flinched and jerked along the ground. Then the shots stopped, and Dickie was still.

Brent looked around. Al Redmond stood there, his gun in his hand, glaring at the little gunman.

'I reckon that evens things for Kyle,' Redmond said. He looked at Brent. 'I'd have shot him sooner, but I was afraid of hitting you.'

Brent knelt beside Dickie. There was no life left in the gunman. 'Wish he could have told us how many men Patzel had.'

'He'd have lied about it if he could have talked,' Redmond said.

'Probably so,' Brent agreed. 'I owe you my life, Al. When he fell, I was too far away to stop him from getting his gun.' He turned to Rosene. 'Are you hurt?'

Rosene shook her head. 'He said he was going to kidnap me and exchange me for the horses.'

Brent nodded, moving over to Rosene. 'We should have thought of that.'

'Would it have worked?' Rosene asked.

Brent sighed. 'It sure would have. He'd have gotten the horses without another shot being fired. We'll keep a man with you women from now on.'

'Nobody will sneak up on us again,' Rosene promised. 'We need one of the dogs here in camp.'

Brent nodded. 'I guess so.' He moved closer to Rosene. 'Are you sure you're all right?'

Suddenly she was in his arms, and Brent detect a sob in her voice. 'I was scared to death,' she whispered. 'I don't know what I'd have done if you hadn't been there.'

He held her close.

'It wasn't all one-sided,' he said. 'If you hadn't rammed that elbow into his stomach, I'd never have reached him before he got his gun in his hand.'

'I hate to break anything up,' Redmond interrupted, 'but if Dickie could sneak down off those bluffs into camp, other men can, too. We'd better keep an eye open.'

'You're right,' Brent agreed. To Rosene, he

said, 'Better stick close to the others. I'll be back in time for supper.'

'Where are you going?' Rosene demanded.

'I want to find out what Patzel is doing. He won't give up.' He looked up at Redmond. 'Keep an eye on things here.'

He glanced up at the sky. Twilight was touching the rims of the little canyon now, but the dusk was deepening rapidly down on the floor. Brent moved away from the wagon, studying his surroundings. He hadn't seen any of Patzel's men except Dickie for nearly an hour now. He didn't believe they were up there on the rim, just waiting for someone to show himself down below.

Sure that no one could detect his movements in the brush, Brent made his way cautiously toward the mouth of the canyon. There was only one way into this canyon and only one way out. Brent guessed that Patzel had already sealed off the escape route.

Every few seconds, Brent paused to listen. It wasn't until he was nearing the brush-choked mouth of the canyon that he heard anything. He stopped there for a full minute and listened. Patzel's men were spreading out across the mouth of the canyon.

'Move up,' one man said loudly enough for Brent to hear. 'The canyon is narrower up ahead.'

'They can't get past us now,' a man closer to Brent said. 'If they want to slip out, let them go. They can't get the horses past us.'

'Boss says to keep them trapped here,' the first man said, his voice louder.

'All right,' the first man grumbled. 'But I sure ain't looking forward to a night out here in this brush.'

Brent had heard enough. He retreated quietly. If the men were going to advance into the canyon, he had to get out of the way.

Brent heard the brush popping as the men moved forward.

He moved back faster. He'd be a dead man within seconds if he were discovered.

CHAPTER SIXTEEN

Brent was convinced now that the attack would start at dawn, just as soon as Patzel and his men could see well enough to shoot straight.

Back close to the camp, Brent stopped. Patzel's men would have halted back at the narrowest place in the canyon. The walls were almost perpendicular right at that spot and were closer together than at any other place. A mouse couldn't squeeze past those men without being detected.

Brent heard Mrs. Hanson call to Morrie and Redmond to come and get their supper. Brent hurried into camp. He'd have to come up with some plan, or at dawn they'd have a fight on their hands that they had no chance of winning.

'Where have you been?' Redmond demanded as soon as he showed up in the circle of firelight.

'Checking on Patzel's men,' Brent said.

Morrie glanced up at the darkened rim of the canyon. 'You been up there?'

Brent shook his head. 'I was down to the end of the canyon. That's where they are now.'

'If they're that close, how come they didn't charge in here when I shot Dickie?' Redmond asked.

'Maybe Patzel didn't know that Dickie had come down here, or maybe he figured that what happened to Dickie was his own business,' Brent said. 'What did you do with him?'

'Rolled him in a blanket and put him over there under the rim,' Redmond said. 'Do you think they'll sneak in here during the night?'

'I doubt it,' Brent said. 'I got close enough to hear them talking, although I didn't see any of them. They're going to make sure we don't slip out during the night; then they'll hit us about dawn.'

'How many?' Morrie asked.

'I can only guess,' Brent said. 'But it sounded like a lot. Maybe fifteen or twenty.'

'We don't have a chance,' Hanson moaned.

'Not if we play the game according to their rules,' Brent admitted.

'Do we climb out of the canyon tonight?' Rosene asked. 'We would make it.'

'We couldn't get a horse up there,' Brent said. 'How far do you think we'd get in this country afoot, especially with Patzel's men looking for us? And they would look for us just as soon as they found we were gone. Patzel doesn't want anybody telling what happened here.'

'What will we do?' Morrie asked.

'Patzel won't do anything till morning,' Brent said. 'Let me chew on it awhile. Soon as we finish supper, put out this fire. Morrie, you take that dog and keep watch down the canyon from here. If any of Patzel's men get ideas about hurrying things up, that dog will tell you when he gets close. I'm going to go up where Woodie is.'

Half an hour later, Brent reached Woodcock. 'See anything up here?' he asked.

'Peaceful as a church,' Woodcock said. 'Even the dog doesn't hear a thing that oughtn't be here.'

'I don't think there is any danger up here. Patzel aims to strike from the other end of the canyon at dawn.'

Woodcock nodded. 'Reckon that does make sense from his viewpoint. If he hit during the night, the horses would stampede out of here, and he wouldn't be able to find half of them. Once they got out on the river bottom, the Indians would pick them up fast.'

'I think you just hit on the answer,' Brent said. 'Patzel's men are strung across the canyon at that narrow spot between the steep walls. If these horses stampeded out of here, they might catch a lot of those men before they could crawl to a safe place.'

Woodcock whistled softly. 'You are right. When do we start it?'

'Not now,' Brent said quickly. 'Just before dawn. I heard them say they'd hit our camp early tomorrow morning. I'm sure Patzel will wait till he can see what is going on. Not only that, but Patzel isn't with his men now. He will be in the morning though. I want him in the middle of this.'

Woodcock nodded. 'If we can get rid of Patzel, the others won't be so hard to handle.'

'We don't want these horses stampeded all over the country in the middle of the night any more than Patzel does. If we wait till just before dawn, that will give us a chance to gather them up again right away. Maybe we won't lose many.'

'I'd better stay up here with the dog,' Woodcock said. 'They might try something funny.'

'Go get your supper while I stay here,' Brent said. 'Then you come back or send Al.'

Woodcock disappeared but was back in

half an hour. 'They like your idea,' he reported. 'Even Hanson thinks it might work.'

'We'll have to depend entirely on surprise,' Brent warned. 'I'll go back to camp. Think you can sleep some here?'

'Sure,' Woodcock said. 'I'll put my rope on the dog. If anything comes near, he'll wake me up.'

Brent went back to camp and went over plans for the morning stampede with the others. He tried to get some sleep, but it was out of the question. He got up and took his turn patrolling the area between the camp and the canyon mouth to make sure none of Patzel's men got impatient and came too close. The dog kept his eyes on the canyon mouth and growled occasionally, but didn't show any unusual excitement. Brent felt a degree of comfort, just knowing that the dog was aware of the men down the canyon.

An hour before the first streak of dawn was due to appear, Brent came back to the camp. He nudged the others and found that most were already awake.

'Morrie, take the dog and keep watch to make sure nobody comes near. Al, you help me hitch the team to the wagon. We've got to do it without any sound.'

'How will we keep the team from running away when you stampede the other horses?' Rosene asked.

'You and your father will have to hold their heads while we get the other horses running. Then get in the wagon and come right behind them. I don't want you left in here.'

'Keeping them from breaking away before we're ready will be our problem,' Rosene said.

With the team hitched up and Rosene and Hanson at the horses' heads, Brent called to Rosene.

'You and your father will have to hold their heads,' he said. 'Now don't move the wagon till you hear us start the herd,' he warned Hanson. 'Patzel's men will hear the first move that wagon makes. Once the herd starts, get the wagon over against the canyon wall where you had the fire last night. There's a pocket there where the horses won't hit it. Then be ready to come after us as soon as the herd is past.'

Hanson nodded, and Brent looked at Rosene, who was only a dim figure five feet away in the dark.

'Good luck,' she said softly.

'That goes both ways,' Brent said.

He led his saddled horse slowly along the east side of the herd, Redmond and Morrie directly behind him.

The horses were still lying down, and Brent didn't stir them as he moved back to the far end of the herd. There they found Woodcock wide awake. He tightened the cinch on his horse and removed the rope from the dog.

'Sure been quiet back here,' he said.

'It won't be much longer,' Brent said.

'Figure they're about ready to hit us?'

'In maybe another half-hour,' Brent said. 'We'll beat them to it. Patzel should be with them now. Let's go.'

Morrie and Woodcock moved to the left, while Redmond swung to the right. When Brent decided they should be in place, he lifted his revolver and fired a shot in the air. Shots to the right and left were almost echoes of his.

Excited whistles split the darkness as the horses lunged to their feet. At the second round of shots, they turned down the canyon and broke into a terrified run. The four riders followed them, shouting and firing another round of shots into the air.

By the time the horses passed the wagon crowded back against the canyon wall, they were running at full speed.

The stampede swept past the wagon, and Brent rode over close enough to see that Rosene and Hanson were leaping into the wagon as the team broke into a wild run after the herd. That much of his plan had worked perfectly.

Brent wheeled in behind the horses. They were making a terrific roar now as their hoofs thundered through the brushy canyon. Ahead, Brent thought he heard a few scattered revolver shots, but he couldn't be sure in all the noise. He was certain that there would be nothing in the wake of that herd to stop him and his men from riding out of the canyon.

Brent dropped back a bit to ride beside the wagon. The horses were running at full speed, and the wagon was bouncing high over the shrubs and brush. He got close enough to see that Rosene had the reins and Hanson and his wife were hanging on for their lives.

The herd funneled through the narrow spot in the canyon and thundered on out into the open river valley. Brent and his men came through the narrow gap, but it was too dark to see what damage the stampede had caused.

Out in the valley, the herd continued toward the river, fanning out as it went. Brent shouted orders to cut around the herd and try to get the horses milling. But he soon discovered this wasn't a cow herd. The horses they were riding were losing ground on the stampede.

But once out of the canyon and recovering from their terror at the sudden explosion of sound at their bedding grounds, the horses soon slowed down and began turning to look behind. Even in the dark, they seemed to sense that the danger was past.

Streaks of dawn were bright in the eastern sky, however, before Brent and his men caught up with the herd. By then, the horses had had enough running and were willing to stop and begin eating. Once the herd was stopped, Brent rode back to meet the wagon. The team was at a walk now, exhausted from pulling the wagon out of the canyon at a dead run.

'Woodie, you and Morrie watch the herd,' Brent said. 'Al and I will check for any strays and see what happened back in the canyon.'

'Better be ready to do some shooting,' Morrie warned. 'No telling what you'll find back there.'

Brent nodded and rode off with Redmond. The canyon was deathly quiet in the rising sun as they rode into the mouth. At the narrowest spot, they saw that their surprise had been very effective. Six bodies were strung across the canyon, trampled almost beyond recognition. However, one of the first ones that Brent rode up to he recognized instantly as Oker Patzel.

'That should take care of our trouble,' Brent said, looking down at Patzel. 'I doubt if his men will have any stomach for going on with the fight now.'

'We've got a big burying job to do,' Redmond said. 'Wonder what happened to the others.'

'We'd better find out before we stop to dig any graves,' Brent said.

Riding along the canyon wall, Brent came on a man who was far from dead. He had a broken leg, and Brent noted that he had no gun. Swinging down, he knelt beside him.

'How many got away?' he demanded.

The man scowled at Brent. 'I'm dying, and you want to know how many got away.'

'You're not dying, or you wouldn't worry about what I'm thinking. We'll fix you up. How many got away?'

'I don't know,' the man said. 'Looked like everybody got killed. There was seventeen of us.'

'That means about ten got away. Patzel didn't make it. Where will the others go?'

'I don't know,' the man said, anger in his voice, and Brent knew he wasn't as badly off as he'd thought at first. 'They'll clear out, though.'

Brent was willing to take the man at his word. A search of the area disclosed another body and another injured man. There was no trace of the other eight.

Brent did what he could for the injured men, promising that he'd come back with the wagon and some medicine. Then he and Redmond took the bodies and laid them against one wall of the canyon. Redmond went up the canyon, brought Dickie's body and laid it with the rest. In a few minutes, they had shoved dirt down from the bluff to cover the bodies so that no predatory animal could find them.

Promising the wounded men they'd be

back, Brent and Redmond rode out of the canyon and to the northwest, where Woodcock and Hanson were holding the herd.

But the moment they came within sight of the herd, Brent reined up sharply. There were a dozen riders clustered around the wagon.

'Looks like we figured wrong about Patzel's men,' Redmond said. 'How are we going to handle this?'

Brent studied the group for a minute; then a grin broke over his face. 'Those aren't Patzel's men. That's my brother Bill and the men he's bringing to help get the horses over the mountains.' He kicked his horse into a run to the wagon.

'Morrie tells me we're just a little late,' Bill Brent said, after greeting his brother.

'You did miss out on some excitement,' Brent said. 'Thought you were going to meet us in Fort Laramie.'

'Heard that Patzel had been through there,' Bill said. 'So I figured what he was up to and came along to help.'

'Patzel's dead,' Brent said. 'Got trampled in that stampede. So did six other men. A couple more are hurt. We'll have to take a wagon back and get them.

'Saw a few horses, too, that broke off from the herd. We'll round them up; then we can move on.'

'Doubt if we'll have any more trouble,' Bill said. 'We've got enough men now to handle things, and Shopay won't try much without Patzel. Going to take the missionaries along with us?'

Brent looked over at the wagon. 'Think so,' he said. 'At least one of them.'

He swung down, and Rosene, who had been watching, came running to him. 'Are you all right?'

He caught her in his arms. 'I'm fine. How about you?'

'Except for being bounced half to death, I'm fine,' she said. 'I'm so glad it's over.'

He tipped her head back to look at her face. 'It's not over, Rosene. For us, it's just beginning.'

She nodded without a word. She understood, and he could see in her eyes that this really was the beginning of something far better than he had ever anticipated.

Photoset, printed and bound in Great Britain by
REDWOOD BURN LIMITED, Trowbridge, Wiltshire